Carl Weber's Kingpins:

Snitch

Carl Weber Presents

Carl Weber's Kingpins:

Snitch

Carl Weber Presents

Treasure Hernandez

www.urbanbooks.net

Urban Books, LLC
300 Farmingdale Road, NY-Route 109
Farmingdale, NY 11735

ISBN 13: 978-1-64556-647-2

First Mass Market Printing July 2024
First Trade Paperback Printing January 2022
Printed in the United States of America

10 9 8 7 6 5 4 3 2 1

Distributed by Kensington Publishing Corp.
Submit Orders to:
Customer Service
400 Hahn Road
Westminster, MD 21157-4627
Phone: 1-800-733-3000
Fax: 1-800-659-2436

Part One

Prologue

Vicky

"Raul, please stop! Leave me alone! I promise I won't tell. *Mami*! Leave me alone, please!"

Raul was my stepfather, and a man of God. To the Hispanic community in the South Bronx, he was known as Reverend Raul Lopez, a respectable man who preached the gospel. Those people were a bunch of assholes who were spooked the fuck out by some blue-eyed devil the white man had sold to us as Jesus.

Behind closed doors, Raul was a pervert who loved to molest little boys and girls. He started raping me when I was fourteen years old, the minute I started getting a little bit of ass and tits.

My mother decided to ignore what was happening right under her nose, because she was suffering from a serious case of low self-esteem. When I tried to tell her, she said, "If you mess this up for me, I will send you to foster care. Got it?"

In her mind, if Raul left her, no one else would want her. She sacrificed her only child for the affection of a muthafucka who didn't give a fuck about her.

"*Mami*! *Mami*! *Mami*!" I screamed for my mother's help.

"Shut the fuck up! Your mama ain't gonna help you!" Raul hissed.

"*Mami*!"

I felt a burning sensation between my legs. Blood was running down the crack of my ass. I closed my eyes and prayed for this ordeal to be over. When he was finished, he pulled his pants up and walked out my room with a Bible tucked under his arm.

For the next week after that horrific experience, I couldn't walk, eat, or sleep. I was ashamed of myself. I couldn't look at my mother in the eyes. I refused to look at myself in the mirror.

Why me? Why me? I asked God over and over again. *Why? I've been good to* Mami*! I've been good in school, I don't cuss! I hate you, God! I hate you!*

Raul's voice kept floating in my head. For three months straight, Raul raped me twice a day.

A few weeks later . . .

My mother and I took a cab from Longwood Avenue to Lincoln Hospital, where doctors examined me and concluded that I wasn't a virgin. While I lay back on the examining table, I felt violated again as a Puerto Rican doctor looked at my pussy in front of my mother.

After hearing I wasn't a virgin, my mother insisted I get a pregnancy test. She didn't even ask me who I'd slept with. She knew who had impregnated me.

"Is she pregnant? I want to know," she barked.

"Let's have a look," the doctor said. He wheeled on his stool over to the ultrasound machine. He fired it up, put some jelly on the end of the wand, and pressed it against my belly.

We all stared at the screen. It looked like a bunch of gray and black splotches. Every time he pressed the wand, the screen would move with it.

"Ah, there it is." He pointed to a spot on the screen. "Right there."

There was a small gray speck on the screen, where he was pointing.

"What am I looking at?" my mother said.

"A fetus."

"What's that?" I asked.

"A baby," said the doctor.

That explains why I'm vomiting everything I eat, I thought.

"Thank you, Dr. Whitaker," my mother said.

"Mrs. Lopez, I know a few clinics that could take care of this," Dr. Whitaker said.

"No! I don't believe in abortions! Thank you, Dr. Whitaker." My mother grabbed my hand and dragged me out of the room. I stumbled as I tried to keep up with her.

I can't believe she's gonna make me keep the child of a rapist. I wanted to scream at her, but just as when Raul was raping me, I couldn't get my mouth to work.

Being the religion freak my mother was, the bitch kicked me out on the street after my seventh month of pregnancy. You know, it was common for those in the church to turn their back on a young girl who'd been raped. As they saw it, she had had premarital sex, and even though they were all committing adultery, sex outside of marriage was a sin. A bunch of hypocrites.

For the remainder of my pregnancy, I crashed on top of the Jackson Avenue rooftops or under the steps of the 149th Street train station. Sometimes, I would just hop the six train and ride all night.

During the day, I sold pussy down in Hunts Point. By the end of the day, I was exhausted. I was turning tricks nonstop. Pregnant pussy was always a hot commodity, because it was always wet.

After I gave birth to my son, Rashad, the state of New York wanted me to put him up for adoption because I was a minor without a stable home. But my best friend, Destiny, and her mother, Carmen, came to the hospital and took custody of my son.

Carmen was a worn-out prostitute who made a hustle out of everything she engaged in. On the surface, rescuing me and my son from the hospital might seem like a noble deed, but the bitch had others plans. A month after I gave birth, Carmen became my pimp. She had me on the ho strip and took half out of every dollar I made, and I wasn't making much.

Standing out there for hours without any action was worse than being pregnant and having to fuck all the time. At least I could lie down for a minute while the john had his way. Standing up all day hurt a girl's legs. Before long, I got tired of hoeing and needed a day off.

"Get your ass up. Time to get out and hustle," Carmen called as she stood in the living-room doorway.

"I'm tired, Carmen. I need a day off," I replied, not moving a muscle on the couch.

"What the fuck did you just say?" She cut her eyes at me.

"I don't want to trick today. I'm tired."

"Don't make me give your son up to the state! You know how them state babies always turn out!"

My baby was the most important thing to me. I was determined to give him a better life than the one I had had so far.

I got up from the couch, threw on my clothes, and got to my corner spot.

I put up with Carmen's threats for three miserable years. When I turned eighteen, I decided I needed to run. One afternoon, while Carmen was taking a nap, I packed my things and grabbed my son. I tiptoed to the front door, opened it as carefully and quietly as I could. When I got outside, I closed the door without making a sound.

With my son in one arm and a suitcase in my other hand, I took off running in the direction of the train station. A train was just about to pull away, and so I sprinted and jumped through the closing train doors. I looked out the window as the train left the station. It would be the last time I looked back on my life. I wanted to forget my childhood.

I found an apartment at the Fox Street shelter in the South Bronx, and there I meet a pretty nigga named Flash, who had a lot of money to spend. This nigga was into that metrosexual shit. Eyebrows shaved, long nails, straight long hair, and a fetish for young pussy. If the nigga were to ever end up in prison, he would definitely have to fight to keep his asshole intact.

"Damn, Ma! What's your name! When did you move in here?" he said to me while I was entering the corner store on Beck Street, a half a block from the shelter.

"Nigga, you too pretty to be spitting out that weak-ass line," I responded, then watched him turn red in the face.

His little crew of young niggas started clowning him.

"Damn, nigga. That bitch just made you look like a fucking nut!" one tall, ugly nigga said. Then he added, "Watch dis! I bet you one hundred dollars she give me some play."

The tall, ugly nigga grabbed a handful of my ass. My reaction shocked everyone standing around. I spit out my straight razor and let it slide across the face of that nigga, giving him a permanent scar.

"Nigga, I bet you a hundred dollars you will never touch another bitch without permission!" I said as I walked away.

"Damn. Dat fucking puta bitch is gangsta," one fat kid said.

"Yo, B, your face is fucked up! That bitch got you real good!" another kid exclaimed.

"Man! Don't tell me my face is fucked up," the tall, ugly nigga said, holding his face, trying to stop the blood.

"Call a fucking ambulance! *Puñeta*, damn it! Get my son some help!" a dark-skinned Cuban chick yelled.

The Fox Street shelter was like a congested prison. People from all parts of the city were crammed on top of each other like rodents in a sack as they waited for Section Eight to place them into one of the city's low-income apartments.

One afternoon, as I was walking down Third Avenue, window-shopping, I felt a gentle hand rub against mine.

"Can I talk to you?" a voice said in a friendly manner.

When I turned around, the pretty nigga I had brushed off three weeks ago at the corner store was standing in front of me with a smile on his face. I instantly spit my razor out my mouth, ready to let the pretty nigga know that I was the wrong bitch to fuck with.

"Do I know you?" I said with an attitude.

"Damn, Ma. You don't remember me?"

"Nigga, what do you want?"

"I just want to talk to you."

"Talk!"

"By the way, my name is Flash. Now, about the other night, don't worry about it. That ugly nigga went back home to Florida. He was just up here visiting his father," the pretty nigga said, as if I was supposed to be impressed with his speech.

"Trust me, my nigga, I'm not worry about anything. I know how to handle myself. But if you feel like picking up his slack, holla at your girl," I said, holding the razor between my fingers.

"Nah, baby, the only thing I wanna do is get to know you a little better."

"That's a better line than the other day," I said with a smile.

"You got jokes, huh?"

"You are a funny nigga."

"Let's go over to my apartment, so I can show you how funny I can get."

"What's that? A challenge?" I asked him.

"Something like that."

"You ain't saying nothing, bet!"

The second we entered his apartment, Flash undressed me, then began sucking my toes. Once he laid me down on his bed, he turned me around and began licking the crack of my ass. I was in ecstasy. I felt like I was in heaven. I pinched my own nipples.

"Give me some dick, nigga!"

Flash stopped sucking my toes and ordered me to get up from the bed. "Stand up and grab your ankles!"

He put his dick inside my wet pussy and then pulled out of me softly. Then he started rubbing his dick against my asshole, stimulating all these nerves I never knew existed. Gripping my waist, Flash stuck it in my asshole, then ground inside my ass, feeling the inside of my walls. The pain was nothing compared to the pleasure that was running through my body. When he was done letting loose, he pulled out, went into the bathroom, and washed up his dick. When he came back into the room, I was lying in bed, playing with my pussy.

"Nah, Ma. You don't have to play with yourself. I'm ready for round two."

That same day we fucked each other's brains out, raw.

Flash turned out to be a typical asshole, broke-ass wannabe pimp, one who wanted to pimp me out. At first, I thought he was the truth, but once I discovered he went both ways, I kicked his ass to the curb.

It all happened when I was out shopping one day and realized I had forgotten my phone. I went back in the apartment to get it before going to a movie. There was a funny smell when I entered the apartment. I stopped to sniff. I heard a noise coming from the back room. I assumed it was Flash and my son playing some wrestling game. I was wrong. I opened the door and saw Flash bent over, getting fucked by a big black guy covered in jail tats.

"Faggot, put your pants on and get the fuck out!" I yelled.

"What do you mean? Come and join in." Flash smiled.

"Hell no. I don't fuck no fags."

Flash finally put his clothes on and left. I never let him back.

The only problem was, I was eight months pregnant with my second child. Once Li'l Flash was born, I bounced from one city shelter to another. At eighteen years old, with two mouths to feed, I was forced to go on welfare.

Walking into the welfare office down on Third Avenue was the hardest thing I had ever done in my life. I had never thought once in my life that my children would become a product of the system. The welfare office was jam-packed, with nothing but Latina and Black faces. I took a number and waited to be interviewed by a social worker. After four long hours of waiting, my number was called on a loudspeaker.

The social worker behind the desk wasn't a friendly person. She had been condescending and rude to the two girls before me. I vowed never to become that mean and angry. It was intimidating to watch the woman berate the people before me, but I was determined to feed my kids, so I swallowed my pride. I felt the river of pain that flowed through my veins.

When I reached her desk, she gave me a "What do you want?" look.

"Hello." I smiled.

"What you need?" She scowled at me.

"Well, I hope you can help me. I'd like to apply for welfare. I have two babies, and I need help feeding them."

"Where is your babies' father at?" she asked condescendingly.

I ignored her. "What are the benefits I'm able to receive? I think I can get SNAP and some money for each of my children."

She rolled her eyes and handed me a piece of paper to sign and an envelope containing sixty-five dollars' worth of food stamps. I took the food stamps without hesitation. I needed them to feed my babies.

"I'm supposed to feed two kids with sixty-five dollars?" I yelled at the social worker. If it wasn't for the Plexiglas separating us, I would've beaten this bitch down.

Walking out of the welfare office, I felt like I'd been raped of my dignity, again, for sixty-five dollars.

Chapter One

Rashad

Life ain't shit. Believe me when I tell you, there's nothing in this fucking world to be thankful for. My mother, La Puta, also known as Vicky Lopez, is a stone-cold hustler who did what was necessary to ensure my li'l brother and I had food on the table and clothes on our backs. I'm the product of a rapist. I was born on my mother's fifteenth birthday.

The streets of the South Bronx raised me. My father was any punk-ass trick willing to break La Puta off with a few dollars. For the first eight years of my life, I had more fathers than I could count. The baker from the bakery down the block. The banker from the bank on 149th Street. The gas attendant, the mailman, the funeral home director, and the store owner. My mother didn't earn the nickname La Puta for no reason. Fucking and sucking were part of her scheme; draining niggas' pockets was her only mission in life.

La Puta was the flyest mom on the block. When the Mister Softee ice cream truck came around, she would pull her bankroll out and buy all the li'l kids ice cream. That was how I hooked up with my niggas. Well, sort of. Actually, Grip, Dirty D, Tungo, and Miguelito were four dirty li'l niggas who stayed in trouble on the block, and I was a li'l fly nigga with all the latest gear.

I was nine years old when La Puta's real father popped up out of nowhere and came looking for her. When he located her, she was down in Hunts Point, slinging rocks and selling pussy. At first when Ricardo approached her, she treated him like a straight trick.

"Rocks or pussy! Rocks are ten! Pussy is forty! Don't waste my time, old head!" La Puta told Ricardo, looking him up and down, trying to see if this well-kept old head was the police or not. "Ain't no window-shopping here, so either you cop or roll."

"I don't think you remember me," Ricardo said, stroking his watch.

"Ma'fucker! I don't remember what I did yesterday. Am I supposed to remember your fine ass or something?" By now my aunt Destiny had joined La Puta in the face-off with Ricardo.

"I guess not! But I'm your father. I know it doesn't sound right, but let me explain. I'm really your father." Ricardo pulled out his wallet and showed La Puta a baby picture of her. The same picture she had up in her room.

"I don't have a father! My father died when I was three years old," La Puta blurted out, not wanting to believe what she was hearing and seeing. She studied Ricardo and couldn't help but notice the similarities. She had Ricardo's jaw, and her eyes were the same as his. She had inherited his curly hair and had his good looks in such obvious ways, but for a moment, she rejected the notion. But even if she wanted, she couldn't deny that Ricardo was her biological father.

"I'm sorry! Your mother took you away from me when you were three years old, but I never gave up hope of finding you one day. I'm sorry!" Ricardo said.

After Ricardo explained to her why he had been out of the picture for so long, La Puta, being the hustler that she was, didn't hesitate to hug him, cry on his shoulder, kiss him on the cheeks, and call him Daddy. As far as she was concerned, Ricardo could be rich. Shit! He looked like money. Even at fifty-five years old, he kept himself in shape, had a fresh cut, and wore Gianni Versace dress-down attire with an eighteen-karat Rolex Presidential watch with diamonds and a fluted bezel on his wrist. And it didn't hurt that he was pushing a new Acura Legend.

It was the summer of 1994, and La Puta, my li'l brother, Flash, and me decided to move into Ricardo's house on White Plains Road in the Bronx. We had hit the jackpot! Ricardo was the proud owner of five barbershops and three clothing stores on Third Avenue. He spoiled the shit out of my brother and me. Since hustling was in my blood, I took advantage of it. I guessed he was trying to make up for the time he had lost with La Puta.

For my tenth birthday, and for La Puta's twenty-fifth birthday, which was a few days later, he treated us to a shopping spree. I picked out the latest Jordans, and I couldn't wait to show them off. Once we returned to Ricardo's house, he blessed La Puta with a birthday card. She opened it. Inside was ten thousand dollars. He handed me a card next, and I opened it to discover two one-thousand-dollar bills. I thought I was rich. At that moment I knew I didn't want to be a broke nigga ever again.

An hour later I threw on my new Jordans and got in Ricardo's Acura Legend and waited for La Puta to get dressed. My adrenaline was pumping. I wanted to front on the block. When La Puta pulled up in front of the barbershop on Third Avenue, I got out of the car and made my way down to the Patterson projects.

I stepped onto the projects' playground, beaming about my new gear. I was a fly nigga with a new pair of Jordans. I knew everyone would be sweatin' me. I swaggered across the blacktop like I owned the block. A group of young niggas sitting on the jungle gym jumped off and came up to me.

The chubby nigga in front said, "Yo, them the new Jordans?"

I smiled. I knew everyone would be envious of my gear. "Yeah. Just got 'em for my birthday."

The chubby nigga punched me in my jaw, stunning me and making my vision blurry. I felt someone push me to the ground. Before I had time to fight back, I was being kicked and punched by six young niggas.

"These sneakers are mine now, nigga," the chubby one told me triumphantly as he pulled the Jordans off my feet. I rolled over and got kicked in my head one more time before they all ran off, laughing.

When I was able to see straight, I ran barefoot back to the barbershop. When I stepped inside and La Puta saw me crying, she smacked me upside my head.

"Listen here, boy! Men don't cry, so don't ever let me see you crying! You hear me? Now take your ass back out there and fight for your shit. Don't come back in here without your shit, 'cause if you do, I'm gonna whip your ass like you stole something from me."

I ran back outside in my bare feet, determined to fight for my shit. I picked up an empty bottle and went back to that playground and approached the chubby kid who was rocking my sneakers as if they were his.

"You like fucking with li'l muthafuckas," I said to no one in particular as I smashed the chubby kid upside his big head with the empty bottle. None of his crew did anything to me. They just stood there, stunned that I had come back with such vengeance.

From that day on, Dirty D, Grip, Tungo, Miguelito, and I became best of friends. We formed a crew called the Terror Squad, and we went around causing trouble. Every day was like a party for us. Cutting school became a daily routine. Getting wet up was our first introduction to the drug game. Soon after that, we became young men who loved each other like brothers, who all fell for the allure of the streets.

The streets of the South Bronx were teeming with fake-ass drug dealers and wannabe niggas. The first taste of some real street credibility came for us when we decided to rob this up-and-coming rap artist named Joey Wack.

As he was taking out cash from his pockets in front of a store one day, I snatched the diamond chain from around his neck. I sold it on eBay but didn't get as much for it as I thought I would. Turned out this nigga was frontin' with fake diamonds. Later in life I learned that most niggas with diamonds around they necks were sportin' fakes. Real diamonds that looked like those cost major dough.

On the day of that robbery, we renamed our crew the Pop Rulers. From that day on, everybody in the South Bronx knew that the Pop Rulers, the original Terror Squad, were a force to be reckoned with.

He went over and sat, and to me, I felt you smell there sampled, died the setting on down by to surprise one

Chapter Two

How Can I Just Kill a Man?

Joe Da Crackhead

On Father's Day in 1997, I checked out the barbershop. *In a few hours from now, I'll be paid,* I thought to myself.

It had been a bad day all around. That morning I had woken up broke, in pain, my nose running and an undisguised hunger for a shot of dope turning my stomach. All morning long I'd patrolled the Union Street Playground, hoping to come up with a bag of dope to ease the pain in my stomach.

Eventually, I'd come across this milk crate in the playground, and I'd stood on top of it and drunk methadone to calm my gut. As I'd stood there, my ears had been bombarded by the sound of moving cars, screaming kids, and police sirens.

I'd watched a few pregnant crackheads coming and going from the dope spot across the street. At the same time I'd checked out Ricardo's barbershop. *A good gig to rob*, I'd thought to myself.

No one trusted my muthafucking ass, and none of the drug dealers on Union Street would give me a free bag, even though it was Father's Day. Them petty niggas wouldn't even cut me a break. Actually, I was a fucking lame, a cold-blooded junkie with no loyalty whatsoever. Nevertheless, I could be an asset to the dealers on the block if given a break. You see, I knew everybody down on Union Street, and I knew every spot. I knew which apartment the police used for surveillance. I was also good at spotting the police from a mile away when they were sneaking around. But since none of the dealers would give me a bag of dope, I never bothered to yell, "Five-oh!" when I saw the unmarked black van pulling up to the rear of the building.

It was also known throughout the neighborhood that Ricardo stayed with a fat bankroll. Plus, he hated the drug dealers who sold dope in front of his barbershop. It was ruining his business.

I saw the perfect opportunity to convince a dope fiend named Sam to rob Ricardo's barbershop with me. I told him Ricardo was the one calling the cops on the dealers on the block. Sam wanted revenge, because he thought Ricardo was fucking up his hustle, so he decided to rob the barbershop with me that day.

"I'm going to put a bullet in his head," Sam shouted, looking tense with anger. He screamed out, "*Puñeta*! Goddamn! I need a shot of dope!"

Ricardo was standing over a barber chair, giving his grandson his weekly haircut, when Sam and I walked into the four-chair barbershop.

"What do you want, sir?" Ricardo asked Sam when he saw him enter the barbershop.

"Your life, *pendejo*, coward!" I shouted as Sam pointed his gun at Ricardo, then squeezed the trigger and shot him twice in the stomach. Ricardo tried to kick Sam in the balls, but he didn't prevail: he toppled forward and fell to the floor.

"Don't do this to me. Please don't hurt my grandson!" Ricardo cried out, and then he began to sob from the pain in his stomach.

"Shut up! You fuckin' old bitch!" I responded as Sam stood over him, putting his gun to the back of his head.

"Nooo!" Ricardo's voice was filled with anguish.

A minute later Ricardo lay motionless on the floor, and Sam and I turned our attention toward the person who had jumped on my back. It was Ricardo's grandson. My reflexes jumped in, and I pistol-whipped the li'l nigga in his mouth. Once he was on the floor next to his grandfather, I gave him a sinister smile while Sam went through Ricardo's pockets, taking his bankroll and watch.

"How old are you, li'l nigga?" Sam asked while pointing his gun at the boy's face.

"Twelve!" he responded, giving Sam an attitude by looking directly into his eyes, letting Sam know he wasn't scared to die.

"Do you want to live or die?" Sam barked.

"It don't matter! You're the one with the gun, you fucking coward!" Then the li'l nigga tried to spit in Sam's face.

"I should send you to hell with Granddaddy," Sam told him as he pistol-whipped him one more time for trying to spit in his face. Sam let him know that if he really wanted to die, he could. Sam had no problem shooting a li'l nigga in the head.

"Fuck that, Sam. Kill the little bastard, so we can go cop a shot of dope. I'm sick as hell," I said, looking toward the door.

"I'ma let you live, but if you talk to the police, I'ma kill you and your family," Sam told the kid.

"I'm no snitch," the li'l nigga responded, still looking Sam in the eyes.

We exited the barbershop, as if nothing had ever happened.

Rashad

I reached under my grandfather's neck, lifted his head, and held his head in my arms. I tried to stop the blood that was pouring from the hole in the back of his head. I didn't want him to die. The tears were burning my face. People were standing on the sidewalk, looking into the barbershop, but no one would come in and help. When the police finally arrived, my grandfather had already been dead for forty-five minutes, and a psychopath had been born. That was the last time I ever cried. Everything I had ever loved and respected had been snatched from me right in front of my eyes, and I hadn't been able to do shit about it. Damn! I wished then that I was grown up.

La Puta

During the two years Ricardo had been in my life, it had been all lovely. I was glad to have met my real father, but now he was dead, gone, and I was back to square one, hustling and trying to make a dollar out of fifteen cents. Ricardo left me his house and car. The clothing stores and the barbershops were rented out, and since I had no interest in maintaining them, I sold all the merchandise after his funeral.

Rashad

That day when I held my grandfather in my arms and saw his eyes roll to the back of his head, I vowed to hurt and destroy anything that stood in my path. My mission was to inflict pain on other people. I wanted the world to feel my pain.

These two bitch-ass junkies had murdered my grandfather for eight hundred dollars and a watch, and to satisfy their distorted beliefs. Sam really believed that my grandfather had called the cops on him, when in fact, it was Joe who had called the cops. That information was later revealed in court. Due to the fact that I refused to testify against Sam and Joe during their trial, they both ended up gettin' five to ten years in state prison for an illegal gun charge. They beat the murder rap. La Puta was mad that I didn't help put them away for twenty-five years to life. She couldn't understand that at the tender age of twelve, I had already made plans to murder both of them one day. Their faces became motivation for me to become ruthless toward other people. Them bitch-ass niggas shoulda killed me when they had the opportunity. One day they would regret they had let me live.

Chapter Three

Fuck da Police

Rashad

Two days before my thirteenth birthday, Miguelito and I were arrested for aggravated assault and the attempted murder of a New York City police officer. Officer Camacho used to be one of La Puta's tricks when she was selling pussy down on Hunts Point. La Puta used to break this muthafucka off once in a while with some ass, and in return he would let her hustle.

He was one of those out-of-shape, nasty-looking, breath-stinking-like-shit, fat muthafuckas who sat in his patrol car, drinking coffee and eating donuts all day long. He was also one of the arresting officers who had slapped the handcuffs on Sam and Crackhead Joe when Ricardo was murdered. Since I had refused to identify them or testify against them, Officer Camacho's promotion to sergeant had gone down the drain. From that day on, he had stopped me and my crew whenever he saw us, for no reason at all. He would line us up against the wall, with our hands behind our head, and interrogate us about dumb shit. It had got to the point where we would run whenever we saw a cop car. On several occasions, he had held me upright by my shirt, put his police revolver to my head or in my mouth, and said, "Do you want to go to hell with your granddaddy?"

I was tired of his bullshit, so I strapped myself up with a 9 mm I had found in Ricardo's house and waited for this nasty pig to stop me again.

I was sitting in front of the building Miguelito lived in on Prospect Avenue when I spotted Officer Camacho's unmarked police car coming up the block. Before he could stop us, Miguelito and I ran into the building and waited for the pig in the dark hallway. Everybody in the neighborhood hated him, so no one bothered to warn him that all the light bulbs in the building's hallways were blown out. When he entered the building, I pulled the trigger on my 9 mm and let eight shots out, five to his chest and three to his legs. But he didn't die. The only thing that saved his ass was his police vest. When I saw him go down, I tried to shoot him again in his face, but I was out of bullets. At the same time we heard him shout into his police radio, "Ten thirteen, officer shot at the Union Street projects. Officer in civilian clothes, chasing two male Hispanics armed with a gun." Within seconds, cops surrounded the front of the Union Street projects.

Every cop on patrol in the Fortieth Precinct was in front of the building Miguelito lived in. A fellow police officer had been shot and was requesting assistance. Nothing else mattered to those cops. We heard the deafening sirens and wondered how many of our niggas the police had rounded up, but the only thing that really mattered to Miguelito and me was that we had shot the pig who had kept harassing us, me in particular.

We heard the footsteps of the angry cops who were searching the building for us. We were lying flat on our stomachs on top of the elevator. When they couldn't find us, they brought in the police dogs to sniff us out. Within ten seconds the dogs found us, and those officers pulled us off the top of the elevator. Then Miguelito and I had eight of New York's Finest beating the living hell out of us. They even tried to throw us down the steps.

Suddenly we heard Carmen's voice shouting, "Those are my grandsons. They are only twelve years old!" One of the cops tried to push her away, but another cop realized the news media was nearby and ordered the cops who were beating us to stop. They cuffed us and escorted us to a waiting police car. Everyone on Prospect Avenue surrounded the area and cheered for us when we were brought out of the building. Some yelled, "Fuck da police!" Others yelled, "They didn't do it!" Miguelito and I both smiled when they pushed us inside the car.

At the police station, the cops refused to allow us any contact with Carmen, until she threatened to sue them if they laid another hand on us. Once the police found out Miguelito and I were only twelve years old, they couldn't charge us as adults, like they wanted to. The Juvenile Offender Act stated very clearly that in order for a juvenile to be charged as an adult, he had to be thirteen years old if the case involved murder and fourteen for all other major felonies. They had no other choice but to drop the attempted murder charge.

Miguelito and I were transferred that night to Spofford, one of the worst juvenile detention facilities in the State of New York. Although we knew most of the young niggas there, we also knew this would be a test of our toughness. Spofford was considered the Rikers Island for juveniles in New York, and it was infamous for young niggas blessing other niggas with a buck fifty across their grill. Spofford was a breeding ground for some of New York City's most ruthless niggas. It was also the place where I learned that stabbing a muthafucka was as easy as slicing cheese.

Everybody that came through Spofford was tested, and if you couldn't fight, then you would become an aspiring, wannabe gangsta, main tagged a bitch, and a bitch I wasn't. So from the rip, Miguelito and I had to put our shit down in a very vicious manner.

"Yo, son! Where you from? What size you wear?" I heard the voice but saw no face. Miguelito and I just kept walking through all kinds of steel doors. Finally, upon reaching our destination for the next year, I heard my name.

"Lopez! Cintron! Y'all going to tier one, cell twenty-nine. Welcome home! Y'all won't be shooting no more cops," the CO said. Once we entered our cell, he slammed our cell door shut.

That night we slept on the floor, in a sitting position, because the COs wouldn't give us mattresses, and we weren't about to beg for some, neither. This was their way of retaliating against us for what we had done.

The next morning, when the doors opened for breakfast, Miguelito and I lined up. We heard that voice again. I turned around to see a husky red nigga standing behind me.

"Yo, son! Where y'all from, and what size y'all wear?" The husky red nigga was looking down toward my new Uptowns. It was either fight for my sneakers or walk back to the housing unit barefoot.

"We from the BX, and one size fit all, nigga!" I responded, jumping on his ass.

We tore it the fuck up fiercely like two animals. A crowd of young niggas cheered us on, while Miguelito held his post, ensuring no one jumped in. Just as I was about to bash this nigga's head against the floor, two COs ran down the corridor, yelling, "Cut it the fuck out!" several times.

As the crowd of young niggas dispersed, Miguelito reached down to my opponent on the floor and stabbed him with a pencil in the neck. Blood squirted from his neck like water from a water fountain. Everyone was locked in their cell until the COs could figure out who was responsible for putting a stop to the Spofford bully. Blaze, as he was known, was serving a juvi life bid, five years, and was considered a young gun, that is, until he bumped his head and thought he could take my shit. Conversations among the inmates could be heard up and down the tier.

"Yo, B! Son put a vicious ass whipping on Blaze," one inmate commented. "I told y'all dat nigga Blaze was a pussy. He just big and ugly. Dat's what he gets for picking on a small nigga."

"Nah, son! We gonna holler at shorty as soon as they crack these doors! God gonna handle its business!" someone else said.

"Nigga, stop fronting! Y'all BK niggas ain't gonna do shit to shorty! I got my money on the young nigga!" another inmate responded.

Laughter broke out throughout the tier.

Slashing and other violence occurred at Spofford on a regular basis. It was the norm, especially if you came in with a pair of sneakers someone else wanted. A nigga's fighting game would determine if he got to keep his shit or not.

The next day, when the lockdown was over, everyone was waiting for the Five Percenters to retaliate, but when they didn't, I guessed they had had second thoughts about fucking with me or Miguelito.

Miguelito and I spent our time working out every single day. Push-ups, crunches, pull-ups, and pumping iron became our daily routine. Eight months into our bid, we were ripped the fuck up, physically and mentally prepared for the mutha-fucking world.

We were released from Spofford exactly a year after we got arrested, with no education and an appetite for destruction.

Besides our mothers, I didn't think anyone cared if we were out of jail or not. Union Street was the same. The projects were still infected with bugs, and New York City with rats. No hot water or heat, just like before. Half of the buildings on the block were still empty, boarded up with plywood, littered with graffiti, and taken over by drug addicts. The street corners continued to serve as open-air drug market for suburbanites looking for their fix. But now Dominicans were running shit on the block, which didn't sit well with me, because if anyone should be profiting from the block, it should be the niggas who had put in work and kept other niggas from invading our block, and those were not the Dominicans. Shit was about to change.

Chapter Four

From Boys to Men

Rashad

Growing up in the South Bronx wasn't an easy task. Today you were alive; tomorrow you could end up dead under some steps, with a bullet hole between your eyes. It was kill or be killed. Become a victim or be the victimizer, the choice was yours. I was determined to play the role of mad child in the promised land.

When Miguelito and I were released from Spofford, my crew, the Pop Rulers, were at war with the Jamaicans over a drug corner, and there was no compromising. If you were from Union Street or Prospect Avenue and got caught in the Bombaclot Jamaican neighborhood, that would probably be your last day on earth, because they were going to kill you, the same way we would've killed one of them if we'd caught them on the wrong side of the street. Murder was the name of the game! The Puerto Ricans were playing for keeps. A homicide for a homicide. Kill one of our friends, we kill two of yours.

The war with the Jamaicans turned really fierce when Freddy Ramos was killed. Nobody really knew the exact details of how Freddy Ramos had ended up on top of the roof of an abandoned building in Brooklyn. Rumors on the street were he had got caught riding the five train, and the Jamaicans had kidnapped him, put him in the trunk of a car, driven him to Brooklyn, and killed him. They'd broken his neck, slammed his head against the concert floor, and plucked one of his eyes from its socket. When his body was discovered, his tongue was swollen in the corner of his mouth, both of his hands were tied behind his back, and he had a gaping slash that stretched from ear to ear. He'd been stabbed over seventy-five times, and even his dick had been cut off and stuffed down his throat. The funeral had a closed casket. This was a reminder that there was a gang war going on over drugs.

Until this point, no one in my crew had a reputation for catching bodies. We were known for viciously beating muthafuckas down. But with Freddy Ramos's death, it was time to put up or shut up. As the leader, I had to set an example for the young niggas under my wings. I was a young star on the rise, so backing down wasn't an option.

Tonight I'm gonna prove my own gangster. I'm gonna see if I'm cut out for this shit. Somebody gotta die! I thought to myself as I sat in the back of a stolen BMW. I was higher than a muthafucka, smokin' wet and ridin' with bad intentions, ready to seize my moment in the spotlight.

As we drove down Longwood Avenue in the South Bronx, I spotted a Jamaican nigga heading toward the train station.

"Hey yo! Park right there!" I yelled at Grip, who was more than happy to obey. Without saying a word, I jumped out of the BMW and headed toward the train station. I was right on the Jamaican boy's heels.

"Yo, my man!" I called. When he glanced back, I said, "Yeah you! Where do I know you from?" I pulled an ice pick from my pocket.

The bombaclot nigga was giving me a stupid-ass look. "Me, uh, don't know you, mon! Me, uh, go catch dah train, mon!"

"You sure you don't know me, man?"

"Me, uh, don't know you, mon! Me, uh, go catch dah train, mon!"

I got right up on him as we entered the station. "Nah, nigga! You ain't going nowhere but to hell, you curry-eating muthafucka." I plunged my ice pick into the dread-headed nigga's heart. He instantly fell down like a rag doll. The dread-headed nigga was dead before he even hit the ground. The only sound I heard throughout the train station was a hissing, like air leaking from a flat tire. No moans. No blood, either.

Shit! This is too easy, I thought to myself as I went through the Jamaican's pockets and robbed him of all he had. "Bitch-ass nigga, you ain't gonna need this no more," I said and snatched the platinum chain with a diamond-studded dollar sign dangling from his neck. Afterward, I kicked his platinum fronts the fuck out of his mouth and pushed his body onto the train tracks.

I walked out of the train station without an ounce of guilt. It was on and poppin'. *Fuck these lame-ass niggas*. The streets of the South Bronx were about to feel my pain.

The Jamaicans retaliated that same night by killing the mother of one of my crew members, Mrs. Cruz. Dirty D's mother had been talking on a pay phone on the corner of 149th Street when a dark blue Toyota Land Cruiser drove slowly up the block. We hadn't paid it any attention, because we'd thought it was some young bucks in a stolen car. Suddenly, bullets had started flying everywhere, like in an attack that could be seen only in a movie. Everyone on the block had scattered.

When the shooting stopped, we'd all come out to inspect the damage. We'd seen blood running down the sidewalk, gun smoke rising up in the air.

And we'd found Mrs. Cruz, a single mother of four, lying on the cold concrete, her body riddled with bullet holes, her blood trickling into the gutter.

The other members of the Pop Rulers knew I was on a mission to demonstrate my murder game was not to be misunderstood. Those who second-guessed us were dealt with accordingly. Each member of the P.R. crew had to catch a body or two. It was simple: get down or lay down. And so the Pop Rulers hit the streets, on a rampage. Niggas who been in the game for a while knew we were young assassins with nothing to lose. After we shut the Jamaicans the fuck down, we ran all the *platano*-eating Dominicans off our block.

Before long an old head from Cypress Avenue peeped my murder game and took the Pop Rulers under his wing. He took a liking to us because we had shot some Queens nigga he was beefing with. Our first encounter with this old head came close to turning into a homicide, because he drove down to our block, looking for me, but no one on the block would tell him who I was or where I laid my head at night. When he finally caught up to me, he was surprised to see I was a young pretty nigga, one who weighed no more than 130 pounds. And most of my goons were a bunch of thirteen- and fourteen-year-olds with double-digit body counts under their belts.

"Hey yo, son! Hop in the car for a minute. I want to holler at you," he said to me as his bodyguard opened the door to his blue Jaguar.

Damn! This nigga is living large for real. I wonder what he wants with me, I thought to myself as my crew of young assassins stood close by, ready to pump some hot pills into this nigga's dome if he or his bodyguard acted funny.

"Nah, old head! If you want to holler at me, you gonna have to get out of the car. I don't ride with strangers."

"You know who I am?"

"I wouldn't give a fuck if you were Jesus! I don't ride with niggas I don't know."

"I like your style. You're sharp! But if I wanted to do anything to you or your crew, I would've done it a long time ago, so be easy, nigga. I only want to talk business with you, that is, if you're interested," he said as he got out of his car. He turned to his bodyguard and signaled for him to fall back and stay in the car.

He went on. "I'll be straight up with you. My name's Blondee. Normally, I don't try to corrupt minors, but in this case, I'ma make an exception. You and your goons are creating a buzz around the Bronx. The streets are fearing the heat y'all dishing out. Niggas in the other four boroughs are speaking highly about y'all's murder game. Supreme and his team out in Queens are feeling some kind of way, because y'all murdered one of his associates. I'm here to offer you and your goons an opportunity to squash that beef before it gets out of hand and, at the same time, to make you and your goons the youngest ballers in the game. No strings attached."

"Old head, I hear what you saying! But I'm no fool. I recognize game when it's being run down on me. Plus, I don't give a fuck about how Supreme feels. Either you keep it funky with me and my niggas, or this conversation is over. What's the reason you want to holla at me? You or your squad don't need me. What's up? I hope you're not trying to set me up!"

My trigger finger was itching. I knew if I bodied a nigga of Blondee's stature, I would definitely be the top nigga in the Boogie Down Bronx.

"Nah! I want you and your goons on my team because y'all young niggas got heart. To survive in dis game, you gotta have heart and balls, and your team got both. If you decide not to, then you can consider me a common enemy, because on the real, the South Bronx belongs to me! I run dis bitch! Dis my muthafucking house. I'm offering you and your goons a once-in-a-lifetime opportunity. Once I jump back in my ride, the offer is dead." Blondee gave me a serious stare. He knew I was raw and rough around the edges, with a lot of street credibility to back up my gangsta. I didn't need no training.

I pretended to think about it for a moment. I knew I was taking his offer. "Deal! But my crew rides with me. If I eat, they eat. And we keep our own block," I said, smiling in his face, showing him I was about business and about my reputation.

"I can only guarantee you three things! My loyalty, respect, and some serious paper. Here is my number." He handed me a card. "Call me tomorrow, so we can arrange to meet and discuss your role in my organization." He hopped back in his car and drove off.

Chapter Five

Young, Dangerous, and Virgins

Rashad

The next day I made plans to meet Blondee at one of his drug houses down on Cypress Avenue. Miguelito, Grip, Tungo, Dirty D, and I arrived strapped to the fullest, not knowing what to expect. When we walked up to the building behind St. Mary's Park, we noticed Blondee's bodyguard standing on the front steps, with a .44 tucked in his waistband. I nodded at the bodyguard to alert my people that he was packing heat. They all nodded their acknowledgment. They'd all peeped the gun.

"Welcome to our home, young blood! Blondee is upstairs, waiting on y'all," Big X, Blondee's bodyguard, announced. He was six feet five, 315 pounds, and ugly. He had spent seven and a half years up North for riding dirty with Blondee. He had taken the case like a man: he'd kept his lips sealed and done his time like a soldier. Even when the alphabet boys had offered him a "get out of jail" card, he'd stood his ground. Upon his release, he'd been welcomed back into the hood with the utmost respect. As a token of appreciation, Blondee had made him the second in command of his organization.

As we made our way to the second floor, I noticed the building was equipped with top-of-the-line surveillance cameras. You couldn't take a step without being seen on camera.

We entered Blondee's immaculate apartment. He was sitting on his couch, smoking a Dutch Masters as a dark-skinned Dominican chick sucked his dick. "Y'all trying to smoke?" Blondee offered up the Dutch.

We were awestruck by what we were witnessing. Although we had a reputation for being young assassins, neither of us had been in some real pussy. We had never seen, smelled, or touched real pussy. But all that shit was about to change for me and my crew.

"Bitch! Hurry da fuck up! And make Daddy come," Blondee said. He mouth fucked the dark-skinned Dominican chick until he felt his hammer knocking her throat loose. When the chick was done swallowing Blondee's nut, she got up from her knees and wrapped her lips around the bottle of Moët that was sitting on the coffee table next to the couch. She downed the Moët and then stood by his side.

"I will smash dat pussy in a minute, Ma! Let me handle some business with my partners here!" Blondee said, slapping the Dominican chick's ass. It shook like freshly made Jell-O.

I just smiled as the girl walked past me, rubbing her fat ass on me. *Damn! Dis is how real ballas get down! I can get use to this*, I thought to myself as I observed all the bitches walking around in thongs. This was the closest I had ever been to pussy, and trust me, I was excited as hell. My dick was rock hard.

Blondee noticed the way my niggas and I were hawking the girls, as if we wanted to rape them. *These young niggas are probably all virgins*, Blondee thought to himself, smiling, admiring the group of young assassins he intended to use to body all his enemies.

"Listen here! You already have your block on lock, so all y'all need is to get y'all weight up. You see this here?" Blondee pulled a brown paper bag from the side of his chair. "This shit here is heroin, dope, da kind of shit fiends will kill for." He looked straight at me. "How much you think dis shit is worth?" he asked me.

"I don't know."

"This is a key of heroin. Dis is worth fifty thousand dollars, with a street value of four hundred thousand tax-free dollars. But for you and your crew, it's free! A gift from me. After y'all get rid of it, y'all can use y'all profit to re-up. I won't hurt you. Y'all part of the family now. I take care of my people. One hand washes the other, right?"

"Right!" I replied.

"Okay! Now, let me show y'all li'l niggas how to cut and bag dis shit up!" Blondee stood up. "By the way, if I catch any of y'all li'l niggas getting high off dis shit, I will personally push y'all wig back, understand me? Dis shit here is only for y'all to get rich fast! Dis is serious!"

For the next six hours, Blondee gave me and my crew a lesson on how to cut and bag up dope.

"That's it. Now you know how to work with this here dope. So what you gonna call your package?" Blondee said.

My whole crew looked at me for the answer. I thought about it for a few minutes, and out of respect for the nigga I'd come up admiring, I decided to use the name that had made George Rivera *the* household name when he was in the drug game.

"Obsession!" I announced.

"I like dat! But you know how much heat them niggas took over that name! The Feds might want to dig in y'all's business about dat name."

"Old head, I'm prepared to deal with all dat shit! I'm riding wit dat name," I said, determined to represent the legacy behind that name.

"I got y'all's back on dat! Y'all niggas wanna party or what? Y'all niggas too young to drink, so all of y'all could go to the back room and get y'all's dicks wet. I got some whores back there waiting to corrupt y'all young niggas." Blondee smiled when he noticed how nervous we were. "I know y'all niggas ain't scared of pussy." He laughed out loud as tears rolled down his face.

"Old head, are you trying to clown us?" Grip asked defensively, feeling like a nut.

"Nah, my li'l nigga! It's just funny to see a bunch of young killas who haven't tasted pussy yet. Dat shit is funny as hell!" Blondee responded, still laughing.

Before he could say another word, his bottom bitch, Vanessa, walked into the room with a bunch of hot whores who were ready to de-virginize my whole crew. Each of the whores grabbed a young nigga by the hand and led him away to a world of lust. We were on cloud nine.

"Y'all niggas ready to get turned the fuck out?" Vanessa asked as she dropped to her knees in front of Grip. His legs were shaking, and his toes were curling up like a bitch inside his Tims. This shit was too real for him.

Blondee caught my eye. "For you, my li'l nigga, I got some exclusive pussy! Don't worry. My girl Fatima goin' take care of you," he said as he waved Fatima over to where the party was jumping off.

When she appeared at his side, Blondee said, "Fatima, dis my li'l partner. See to it dat he enjoy himself properly. Whatever he wants, okay!"

Fatima was an expert at this shit. She was wearing a pair of tight shorts that had her pussy in a choke hold and displayed her swollen entrance, and she had on a wife beater that clearly showed how hard her nipples were. She had a chocolate complexion and an hourglass figure. Her ass was a little bigger than Buffy's. She looked me up and down while licking her lips. *Dis li'l nigga fine as hell. Plus, he got a big dick*, she said to herself when she looked down at my jeans and noticed the print of my dick, which was searching for freedom like a slave in captivity.

"Li'l nigga! You think you can handle all dis ass?" she said to me, grabbing my hand and placing it on her soft ass.

This was the moment of truth, and I couldn't show this whore that I was a virgin. "There's only one way to find out if I can handle all that ass," I said sarcastically.

"I'm ready when you're ready! Let go upstairs to my bedroom, where we can have some privacy," Fatima said before leading me up to her room.

When we got upstairs, Fatima opened the door to her bedroom and led me in, and it was as though we had walked into the Playboy mansion. It had an exotic aroma to it. Her bed was covered with red rose petals, mirrors decorated the ceiling, a plasma TV stood directly in front of the bed. Fatima hit a button on a remote, and the lights in the room dimmed, and a hard-core fucking flick popped up on the plasma TV.

"You ready for some real pussy, li'l nigga?" she asked me as she took her shorts and wife beater off. My eyes almost popped out of my head when I saw Fatima's nipples standing out.

After she sat down on the edge of the bed, she unzipped my pants and pulled them down, and I almost lost control. This shit was too much for me to handle.

"Damn, li'l nigga. Where did you get a dick that big? I'm gonna show you what a bitch could do with a dick this big." She couldn't help herself.

I didn't say anything.

"You want me to stop?" she asked.

I shook my head. "Keep going."

I had no idea what I was doing, so I did exactly what I had seen Blondee do to the Dominican chick. Fatima was the one in control, though.

"Now lay the fuck back on the bed," she told me. Fatima was feeling herself. She was determined to turn my ass the fuck out. Fatima sat her hairy, fat, juicy pussy on my face, giving me a mouthful of pink pussy. Her body was out of control. Her moaning and groaning were all the signs I needed to know that I was doing the right thing.

Fatima was breathing heavily. Twenty minutes later, she came on my dick, while I busted my first nut. Damn! I had never imagined that real pussy was better than my fucking hand. I would never beat my dick ever again, I thought to myself as I watched Fatima's fat ass jiggle on the bed while she lay on her stomach.

Although Fatima was twenty years old, and I was fifteen, age didn't matter. I was instantly addicted to her, and she was more than willing to serve as my teacher, teaching me every position that pleased a whore.

After a few months of running around with Fatima, and after she witnessed how much money a young nigga was banking, I moved in with her. My mother didn't ask no questions, which reinforced my belief that I was the muthafucking man.

Once my mother saw how much money I was getting on a daily basis, she asked to be put on the payroll. Now it was official! Ma dukes was getting her hustle on. She became the South Bronx madam to all the young whores on Hunts Point. It added a steady flow of cash to her bankroll and kept me swimming in pussy.

In every sense of the word, my mother was a diva in her own right. She was brown skinned, weighed 140 pounds, and had cat eyes and a fat ass that had many niggas, young and old, crawling for some of her loving. Even at the age of thirty, she had Sugga Daddy, a strip club she managed in Hunts Point, on smash. Most of the young strippers hated on her, and those who didn't just wanted to be like her: sexy and gangster. La Puta was also known in the South Bronx for giving bitches and niggas alike permanent scars. She didn't hesitate to spit her razor out of her mouth and let anyone feel her gangster.

George Rivera, aka Boy George, from East Tremont, was the South Bronx's biggest drug lord and had a thing for gangster bitches, and La Puta was at top of his list. In my eyes, this nigga was the truth. He was the only nigga I knew that rented a yacht, complete with mad celebrities, for a birthday party. When he would visit La Puta, bitches young and old would throw their panties at him, while broke-ass niggas hated on him from the sidelines. Although the Pop Rulers were officially under Blondee's wing, Miguelito, Grip, Tungo, Dirty D, and I admired the shit out of this nigga. He was the nigga we wanted to emulate. Plus, it didn't hurt that every time he came to my crib to cop himself some of La Puta's pussy, he would let me drive his green Lamborghini Diablo. He was the one who had taught La Puta the art of transporting heroin to D.C., Chicago, Philly, Miami, Detroit, and Puerto Rico. La Puta had a slew of whores who would stuff their pussies with heroin, suck a dick, or get fucked up the ass at the same time. The dope I was getting from Blondee for pennies on the dollars . . . well, La Puta was tripling it in other cities.

Miguelito

We reached kingpin status in a matter of months. Rashad made sure that everybody was taken care of evenly when it was time to collect our share of the profit. With the top-quality heroin Blondee was supplying, we had the entire city on lock. It was nothing to see rap artists, singers, music producers, lawyers, doctors, and politicians down on 149th Street, copping themselves some Obsession. I mean, the same celebrities you normally saw on MTV were blowing my phone up. In fact, one of my best customers was the self-proclaimed king of R & B and his famous wife. Given that they were big spenders, we gave them the red-carpet treatment and delivered their product to them. They always bought weight, so it was smart business for us to accommodate them.

One particular day, the self-proclaimed king of R & B tried to cop with no money We were accommodating to them only to a point. We weren't about to give away product for free.

"Since you got no money, how about you get your wife to suck our dicks?" Dirty D said.

His wife chimed in, "You little niggas wish. I ain't about to suck no one's dick right now."

The king of R & B pursed his lips and shook his head.

His wife slid off her wedding rings and handed them to me. "This should be enough for three grams. You can hold these until next time, when we get you your money."

I handed her the dope. She took it and slid me her home number.

Once a week after that, I drove to her New Jersey home to drop off three to four grams of dope. While the R & B king was running around like he was still hot, I was up in his house, in his bed, smashing his wife's pussy into submission. To me, she was nothing but a high-priced whore who had traded her fame for a taste of the devil's dick. And since I was the devil in the flesh, why not let her blow some high notes on my dick? To me she would always be known as "*Papi, please hit this pussy from the back while I snort this dope.*" The same way America was obsessed with her angelic voice, she was obsessed with snorting Obsession.

Even though we kept a low profile around the neighborhood, we still attracted professional stickup kids who thought they could get off on us.

One day we were on the block, a typical day. Fiends were steadily coming by to cop. There were no problems; everyone was relaxed.

Dirty D was dealing with a fiend when I noticed a new face strolling down the block. Something didn't seem right, and the hair on my neck stood up. This young buck was trying to look like a fiend, but I could tell by his brand-new Tims that he was frontin'.

I was immediately ready for whatever ensued. I put my hand on my 9 mm in my waistband. As he approached, I saw him reach into his coat pocket. Before he was able to get the gun all the way out, I was on top of the nigga, with my gun to his head. Miguelito saw the commotion and jumped in. He knocked the gun from the stickup kid's hand. We both began beating his ass as Dirty D kept the fiends away. We left the nigga bloody and beaten.

"Don't you never come at the king again!" I shouted.

The stickup kid ran away, holding his head, trying to stop the bleeding.

For the most part, business was sweet. We were raking in a quarter of a mil a day. We had storage places in Philly, Delaware, New Jersey, and the Bronx, all of them packed with boxes of money. So if the Feds ever decided to run up on us, they wouldn't find shit. The only items we owned that were worth some cash were our diamond chains, the ones with the P.R. sign. To the naked eye, we were a bunch of li'l niggas who were just trying to eat, but all the real ballers around the city knew we were young, fly, and dangerous. Not bad for a bunch of li'l niggas from the Bronx who just eight months ago were killing mutherfuckas for fun. For every nigga we bodied for Blondee, he blessed us with a key of heroin. In the drug game there were no innocent bystanders. Everyone was fair game.

Chapter Six

Exposed

La Puta

"I don't believe dat no-good faggot did this to you. I swear, I'm going to kill him!" I held my youngest son, Flash, in my arms while he bled from his butthole. Carmen's boyfriend, Robert Jones, had raped him while I was out making a dope drop. This no-good nigga was gonna pay for this shit. If he thought he gonna get his freak on with my son and not suffer any consequences, he was wrong. I should just beat Carmen the fuck up, because at the end of the day, it was her fault. How the fuck she gonna just leave my son in the bedroom with a nigga who had a shady background? While she was in the kitchen, cooking this no-good nigga lunch, he was in the bedroom, fucking my son in the ass. He probably would've killed Flash, but thankfully, Destiny walked in on him and beat his ass with a baseball bat until he was half dead. When the police arrived, Robert Jones was laid out on the floor, unconscious. He was taken into custody and charged with sexually assaulting a minor.

Rashad

I personally made a promise to my li'l brother, Flash, that I would get Robert Jones for raping him, but he brushed me off. "You don't have to. My daddy is gonna get him, because he loves me."

The mere mention of his daddy used to enrage me, because his daddy did, in fact, love him and took care of him. I guessed I could say I was a li'l jealous. I had never had the opportunity to know my real father. I believed this was the reason I had so much hostility inside me. The flip side of that was his daddy was a faggot, one who loved to play the bitch role in a relationship. My brother, Flash, had a lot of his daddy's tendencies. Even though he acted like a li'l bitch, I loved him and protected him. After all, we had been spit out of the same pussy.

Four years later . . .

It was a quiet night on 149th Street. I sat in my car across the street from the train station. I had come here to clear my head. I liked to watch the people enter the station, and hear the trains rumble past. I found it calming and almost relaxing . . . until I'd start thinking about all the shit I needed to do to keep my business on top.

I heard a train enter the station, then pull away. It was moving on to the next stop, transporting people all over the city. Whenever I heard a train, I knew I'd see people exiting the station. On this night, I watched the poorly lit stairs to see who had just gotten off the train. A man walking up the stairs came into view. He looked familiar, but it was too dark to make out who it was. When he reached the top of the stairs and the streetlights illuminated his face, I sat up straighter. It was Robert Jones. He stood at the top of the steps, looking around, as if he was waiting for someone or something. I grabbed my trusty ice pick and got out of the car. My juices were flowing. *Hatred* is a soft word for what I felt toward him. I was homicidally enraged. He was busy looking at his phone and didn't see me coming. When I stepped up behind him, my mind went blank as I gripped my ice pick tight.

"Take dis, you muthafucka." I plunged the ice pick deep into his chest. The moans and the cow sounds this man made gave me a great deal of pleasure. His moans agitated me to the point where my blood was burning inside of me. I needed to destroy the monster in front of me.

"You fat pervert, remember my li'l brother?" I said as I continuously plunged the ice pick into his body. He writhed and wriggled on the ground, trying to get away and stop the attack. I stabbed whatever body part I could. His hand, his arm, his leg, stomach, chest. It didn't matter, just as long as I penetrated his flesh. Everything happened in slow motion.

When the police arrived, they couldn't believe their eyes.

"Whoever did this must be put in jail," one of the police officers told the crowd standing around, enjoying the show.

Everyone on Prospect Avenue knew I was the perpetrator of this diabolical crime, but no one really gave a fuck. Well, most people didn't give a fuck. To my surprise, I was snitched on by a deaf nigga, Gismo Gomez, whom I had taken care of on many occasions. He brought the police to the Union Street Playground, where I was chilling with the rest of my crew. Although he couldn't speak, he kept mumbling and pointing at me. The police handcuffed me and charged me with the attempted murder of a prominent public figure and assault with a deadly weapon. I'd be damned! The good old child rapist was now a respectable reverend. This time I made the front page of the *New York Times*, and I made my debut on C-74, the section for adolescent offenders on Rikers Island.

After that, Gismo Gomez became an enemy of the neighborhood. For his Good Samaritan deeds, a ten-thousand-dollar contract was put on his head. In the eyes of those who made crime a way of life, he was a snitch, a rat, a no-good muthafucka. When you lived in an environment where every other person was involved in some kind of illegal activity, you were not supposed to see or hear anything. When you started seeing and hearing too much, you became a problem. A threat to the survival of others. Therefore, someone was bound to take your life.

Miguelito

I want to inflict as much pain as possible on that snitch-ass nigga, Gismo. How the fuck a deaf muthafucka gonna be telling? These niggas nowadays got the game fucked up. I'ma torture that chump-ass nigga until he talk, I thought to myself as I waited for his ass on the twenty-fifth floor of the Jackson Avenue projects. *If the Pop Rulers don't handle this nigga, people on the block might lose the fear they have for us. There is no thinking or feeling about it. Gismo has to be taught a lesson.* After five hours of waiting, I heard the elevator stop, and to my surprise, Gismo walked out, not realizing what awaited him.

I could swear I heard him say, "Oh shit!" when he felt my 9 mm coming down across his face. I knocked him out with two hard blows to his chin with my 9 mm. I was about to put one in his head, but suddenly, another idea came to my mind. I dragged Gismo back into the elevator and took him up to the roof of the projects. I waited a few minutes and then slapped his ass a few times to wake him up. Once I had revived him, I began aiming and shooting at him. I missed him on purpose because I wanted him to jump from the roof. Once I had him at the very edge of the roof, I shot him dead in the head. His body fell backward and off the rooftop.

By the time I reached the first floor, a crowd of incredulous niggas was standing around the body, which just seemed to have rained out of the sky.

"Yo! This muthafucking blunt got me seeing shit!" one bystander said after having felt the impact of the body hitting the ground.

"Nah, nigga! That's a real fuckin' body! I'm out!" said a woman who was smoking a blunt with a Mexican kid. She quickly moved away from the dead body that had rained from the sky.

Gismo Gomez's death was classified as a suicide by the New York medical examiner. No one really cared, and no one felt like doing the work it would take to solve the murder, which the death obvi-

ously was. To the streets, he was a snitch, so he had
got what he deserved.

Rashad

Two weeks later . . .

Goose bumps rose all over my body as I stepped
into the courtroom and saw the good Reverend
Robert Jones with his head wrapped up and a
patch over his right eye. I couldn't believe he had
survived my attack.

I deliberately watched his every move. He was
wide eyed and fidgety. He appeared worried. He
caught my eye once and quickly looked away. I
looked at the back row of the courtroom, and it
was full of my niggas. Miguelito, Tungo, Dirty D,
Fatima, La Puta, and even my li'l brother, Flash,
and his daddy were there showing a nigga some
love.

Lisa Star, a prosecutor from the Bronx District
Attorney's office, was assigned to my case, and it
was clear from the start that she hoped to obtain
a conviction. She began her opening statement
with a cry for justice and then promised that she
would prove I was a monster and that I deserved
to be put in prison. What she didn't know was that

my attorney was prepared to break her argument down piece by piece.

"Your Honor, on behalf of the State of New York, I wish to approach the bench," Lisa Star announced when it was clear to her that things were not going her way. I saw the disgust on her face and smiled.

My attorney, Linda Williams, approached the bench as well.

"Your Honor, the star witness in this case committed suicide two weeks ago and—"

"Wait a minute, Ms. Star," Linda Williams said quietly. "You have no case without a witness. Why don't we save the taxpayers of this city some money and have your office drop all charges against my client?"

"No! It's not going to be that easy!" Lisa Star yelled, catching the attention of the entire courtroom.

"Your Honor, to proceed with this case without a witness is an injustice to my client." Linda Williams shook her head with a smile.

"Your Honor, the people are prepared to move forward. We have enough evidence against the defendant to proceed."

"I will allow the State to present its case!" said the wrinkle-faced white judge. He looked over at me and gave me a stern look.

"The State calls Reverend Robert Jones to the stand," Lisa Star declared when she returned to her desk.

Reverend Jones took his time approaching the stand. He looked apprehensive, almost as if he didn't want to be there. Lisa Star began her questioning.

"Reverend Jones, where are you from?"

"I'm from the South Bronx."

"How old are you, sir?"

"I'm forty-five years old."

"What do you do for a living?"

"I'm a reverend. I counsel youth at risk."

"Is the person who attacked you in the courtroom today?"

Reverend Jones nodded his head without uttering a word.

"Can you please point him out for the record"? Lisa Star requested.

The good old reverend pointed at me, but he knew he would be exposed. His profile was about to become a matter of the public record. I was smiling, confident I had done the right thing. *I shoulda killed him!* was the only thought that ran through my mind. My demeanor was that of a savage. I didn't avert my gaze from him. I wanted him to remember my face every time he looked in the mirror, just like my li'l brother remembered his.

"Let the record show that Reverend Jones pointed to the defendant, Rashad Lopez," the prosecutor said with a smile. She went on with her questioning. "Reverend Jones, could you please tell us in your own words the event which took place on the third day of November, two weeks ago?"

"I was getting off the six train at a 149th Street, going to visit an old friend."

"Then what happened?"

"I was . . . I was . . ."

"Reverend Jones, would you like a drink of water?"

"No, thank you."

"Reverend Jones, do you know the defendant in this case?"

This was the moment my lawyer was waiting for. The prosecutor had opened the door for my lawyer to step through and expose the reverend. Breathing heavily, the reverend took a long pause. After sipping from the same cup of water he had moments ago refused, he took a deep breath. No one in the courtroom expected his next answer.

"Yes! I know the defendant in this case. He—he's the brother of a kid I was accused of molesting five years ago, before I became a reverend. I would like to ask Your Honor to please drop all the charges against this young man."

The packed courtroom was stunned. The spectators who had come to support the reverend were now crying for my release. The hypocrisy they were displaying was enough for me to see how fucked-up society was spooked by religion.

This nasty-ass reverend had busted my li'l brother's asshole open! Had made my li'l brother suck his dick and had put my li'l brother's dick in his godly mouth. Now he was counscling at-risk youth. I could just imagine how many other kids he had molested while preaching the Word of God. *Fuck him*! I thought. I shoulda killed him.

"The State of New York now drops all the charges against Rashad Lopez. You are free to go home, young man!" declared the wrinkle-faced judge. He turned his attention toward Reverend Jones, who was still sitting on the witness stand.

"Mr. Jones, I'm ordering this court to conduct an investigation into why you are counseling at-risk youth. I want to ensure no other kids are being molested by you." The judge gave the good old reverend a disgusted look.

My crew in the courtroom was celebrating as if we had won the Super Bowl. Fatima, Blondee, La Puta, Miguelito, and Tungo were all talking shit to the reverend's family. La Puta actually had to be held back, because she wanted to jump on the reverend. He had to be escorted out of the courtroom through a side door.

My li'l brother, Flash, sat in the back of the courtroom with his faggot-ass daddy, acting like a Goody Two-shoes, with his punk panties up the crack of his ass.

"They shoulda kept your ass in jail for what you did!" Flash said to me as I walked up to him.

"Bitch-ass faggot! I did that for you!" I stormed. "Where was your punk-ass daddy when you was getting fucked in the ass? Get the fuck outta my face with that sucka shit!"

La Puta saw how enraged I was, and got in the middle of us to prevent me from whipping his ass right in the courtroom. That was last time I spoke to my brother. The next time we bumped heads, I was sure it wouldn't be a nice day for him.

Despite all the evidence the prosecutor had accumulated against me, there was nothing she could do about the charges against me being dropped. Two days later, the good old reverend placed a .38 caliber inside his mouth and blew his brains out while kneeling down next to the Holy Bible. *Amen!*

Chapter Seven

Mo' Money Mo' Problems

Blondee

"How da fuck dis rat-ass, dope-fiend nigga manage to play you for a brick of heroin?" I demanded to know as I sat around a table in my stash house on Cypress Avenue, sweating, veins popping out from the side of my neck, contemplating my next move.

Grip and Tungo stood on opposite sides of me, staring at each other, not knowing if they would have to shoot their way out of this mess, scared to death that they had got caught slipping.

"Trust us! We gonna take care of dat nigga. We know where his baby moms lives. Willie musta forgot the rules to dis game. Babies' moms, fathas, mothas, sistas and brothas, and even babies are not excluded from dis shit. Dat nigga gotta go!"

Miguelito said, his voice tinny. His lower lip trembled slightly. His expression was one of total anger.

I took a long moment before commenting. I put my hands down on the table, fixing Miguelito with a stare. "Dat's not the point, young buck! Da damage is done. You let a known snitch in your cycle, which could only put a dent on our shit, and put our whole operation in some serious danger. I have no doubts that y'all li'l niggas are gonna handle dis mess! But keep in mind, Willie knows y'all's next move! He knows too much. Da streets are talking! Muthafuckas are expecting for y'all to react. For now, y'all must take the L and plan carefully on how to get back at dis nigga."

Rashad

I stood in a corner of the room, listening to Blondee drop some jewels on my two li'l niggas so they could build their own crown. I was prepared to go to war with Blondee if he even acted like he wanted to cause any harm to my niggas. Even though they had violated the rules, rules they had helped create, I wouldn't go against them. We had come into the drug game together, and we had made a pact to leave it together, dead or alive.

But as the leader, I had to put up a good front to keep Blondee calm.

"Listen! I'm not having dis shit!" I barked. "The possibility exists dat nigga might get scared and run straight to the alphabet boys. I would hate to be the one to bury y'all two asses."

Miguelito gave me a funny look, then said, "Oh, really?"

"Y'all two niggas fucked up big-time! But we can fix dis! Willie is not to be touched at all, at least not now. He's probably expecting for us to come looking for him, but we will not! He knows who he's fucking with. Yet he decided to run off with our shit. We gonna send all these dirty-ass clowns out here a message. Muthafuckas get all emotional when you bring family into the picture. We gonna get at his baby mom and mother. By the way, I'm not taking a loss! Y'all two niggas will be paying for dat brick out y'all's pocket. I want my money today! Street value!"

Blondee

Dis was why I had put him on my team! I hoped he didn't bring no heat on his team. Everyone in the South Bronx knew that the Pop Rulers were under my wings. Every move they made only added more credibility to my team. Me personally, I was just acting hard, fronting, like I was mad Willie burned them. What was a key of heroin to a muthafucka that got boatloads of it? I was willing to let certain shit slide if I was handling business myself, but since I was the boss, I got to front like I deserved to be the boss. If these li'l niggas detected that I was pure pussy at heart, I had no doubt they would body my ass.

Miguelito

I guessed Biggie Small said it best: "Mo' money mo' problems." Because the more money the Pop Rulers generated, the more problems we had to deal with on a daily basis.

Tungo

We followed Willie's baby mom and mother for a week straight. We had their daily routine down to a science. Willie's mom was out there, so she was easy to catch up with. If it wasn't for the mission I was on, I would've laid some serious pipe down on Willie's mom. I can't front, for an old head bitch, she definitely had it going on. Her ass was so phat and round, a nigga could set a cup on top of it. The word on the street was that she gave some incredible brain.

Willie's baby mom, Tiffany, parked her beat-up Mazda in front of the Banco de Ponce at 149th Street and Prospect Avenue. She got out of the car and slammed the door shut, leaving Willie's mother in the front passenger seat, sucking on a lollipop. As soon as Willie's baby mom entered the bank, Miguelito and Rashad went around the car. They both carried an iron pipe in their hand. Dirty D and I served as lookouts.

"Bitch, get da fuck outta da car now!" Miguelito ordered as he peered through the window at Willie's mother, but she paid him no mind and kept smacking her lips against her lollipop.

Before she realized what was happening, Miguelito reached inside the car through the passenger window and hit her with his iron pipe on the right side of her face. "Suck on dis, bitch!" he shouted.

She screamed out in panic. However, on Prospect Avenue those kinds of screams were routine, so no one paid her any attention. As far as people were concerned, it was some domestic shit going down, or a pimp was whipping on some whore ass. An unknown strength kept her from moving, and so Miguelito grabbed her by the hair and pulled her out of the car through the window. Her screams abruptly stopped when he knocked her out cold on the sidewalk. Rashad jumped in the driver's seat of the car and popped the trunk open, and then he and Miguelito threw her ass inside it. Afterward, Rashad and Miguelito climbed in the car and waited for Willie's baby mom to come out of the bank. Rashad was in the back seat.

Willie's mother's blood ran freely down the sidewalk into the gutter of an oppressed neighborhood. Her body lay lopsided in the trunk of her daughter-in-law's car. Seeing this bitch's teeth spread out on the sidewalk was a new, gratifying experience. When I spotted Willie's baby mom coming out of the bank, I got an instant hard-on. Violence always did this to me. *One of them bitches gonna get fucked tonight*, I thought.

I was sure Tiffany urinated on herself when she jumped into the driver's side of her car and saw Rashad's and Miguelito's faces. I stepped closer to the Mazda so I could watch the scene unfold.

"Bitch, drive! Don't make this a homicide," Rashad said from the back seat. He was ready to put an end to the bullshit.

"Niggas! Y'all can have the car, the money, whatever y'all want! Just don't hurt me," Tiffany cried.

Bitch, are you serious? Who da fuck want dis beat-up car? I thought. By the way Rashad was staring at her, I could see she knew this wasn't no carjacking.

"Bitch, shut da fuck up and just drive," Rashad barked and then put his FN P90 submachine gun to the back of her head. "Don't hit no bumps. The trigger might go off."

Tiffany

Damn! Where the fuck is Vivian at? I hope she's getting help. How the fuck she just gonna bounce and leave me! Fuck it! These crazy-ass niggas don't need two of us. I hope I can fuck or suck my way out of this shit.

I cranked the steering wheel around on Jackson Avenue and then headed down a narrow street. The nigga with the gun to the back of my head instructed me to park behind a deserted toy warehouse, one that had seen its share of unsolved murders through the years.

Maybe I can try to run. Damn! I'm not trying to get shot! I thought to myself as the nigga in the front seat dragged my ass out of the car quickly. The other nigga in the back seat popped the trunk open and pulled Vivian out by the hair. Before she could get a word out of her mouth, he slapped the shit out of her, knocking her down to the ground. She balled up into a fetal position. Before she could catch her breath, Rashad had her inside the warehouse, trussed up on a bondage rack, handcuffed. She struggled frantically, but to no avail. Rashad shuddered with delight. The thought of what he was about to do to us had him pumped up. The look in his eyes spelled death.

Rashad

This warehouse was favored by the Pop Rulers for torturing muthafuckas who got out of line. A river of pleasure gushed through me and warmed my heart as I observed Willie's baby mom and his mother.

"Yo, strip both of them bitches down, tie that one to the steel beam over there, and tie the older one to a chair. I want her to have a front-row seat to show her what I'm about to put on for her," I said to Miguelito and Tungo.

"Why is you doing dis to us? We don't even know y'all," Tiffany cried after she was tied up.

"Bitch, you don't have to know me. I know you. Trust me, by the end of the day, you will get the opportunity to know me. Right now, since you want to run your mouth, you're the one who gonna pay the price for fucking with a nasty nigga like Willie. Baby, dis the price he must paid for being a Judas in my camp."

"So why not kidnap his sorry ass instead of us? His mama ain't done shit to y'all! I ain't done shit to y'all!" Tiffany said to me, as if her heartfelt speech was going to inspire me to cut her loose.

"Bitch! Why don't you shut da fuck up? I'm tired of hearing your mouth."

"Can we work something out?" she pleaded.

"Oh, you think dis is a joke. Work something out!"

I grabbed a wooden baseball bat lying against the wall and swung it, delivering a deadly blow to her face. Vivian cringed at the sound of bones cracking and the sight of blood pouring from Tiffany's face. Her face was split in half, exposing broken bones and white meat. Tiffany's body shook while she struggled to loosen herself from the steel beam.

"Oh! You still want to work something out, huh? Did I tell you to move?" I was infuriated that Willie had disappeared with a key of my shit. So I beat his baby mom with the bat as if it was him I was beating. Every time I swung the bat, bones would crack. When I broke her kneecaps, her legs from the knee down turned backward.

"Nigga, did you get dat on tape?" I asked Tungo, who was recording the brutal beating with his cell phone. He confirmed that he had with a nod.

I took perverse pleasure in beating Tiffany until she was motionless. Without a shred of compassion, I continued swinging the bat against her body with renewed vigor. Vivian shook in fear. Once I was done beating Tiffany's ass, I ordered Miguelito to untie her. Her broken body hit the floor with a cracking sound that echoed throughout the ware-house. I can't even bullshit. I was on my own dick.

My crimeys were looking at me in shock when I picked up my FN P90 submachine gun and pulled the trigger, filling Tiffany's body with fifty armor-piercing shells. To ensure the message was loud and clear, I spread what was left of Tiffany's legs wide open and shoved the bat handle deep in her stinky, hairless *chocha*, or pussy.

"Hey, yo, get dis nasty *hija de puta*, dis dirty bitch, outta here. I could care less what y'all do with her ass," I shouted.

My goons wasted no time in wrapping Tiffany's body in plastic bags.

"Crotona Park or Orchard Beach?" Tungo asked me.

"Crotona Park. I want the hood to see what happens when a punk-ass nigga get slick. Throw her ass in the swimming pool."

I'm gonna make dat snake-ass nigga Willie crawl out of the grass. I want him to feel the pain, I thought to myself as I watched Tungo and Miguelito carry Tiffany's body out of the warehouse and then throw her in the trunk of her beat-up Mazda.

Tungo walked over to me and leaned forward. "We be back in forty-five minutes! Whatever you do, make sure dat bitch in there get her grill twisted," Tungo whispered in my ear. "Nigga, I just want to fuck old head in the ass a few times, so save some for me!"

Back in the warehouse, Vivian was losing her fucking mind. After watching Tiffany get broken the fuck up with a baseball bat, she was mentally prepared for the worst.

"I got a surprise for you. Wanna see it?" I said as I unzipped my pants and let my long dick hang loose.

Damn! I can't believe this young boy is gonna rape me. He could be my son, Vivian thought to herself.

"I do whatever you want me to. Just don't hurt me, por favor, please!"

"I would let you suck my dick, but you missing three teeth. Plus, I don't trust you."

"Please don't hurt me!"

Vivian's words only excited me more.

"It's up to you! If you act funny, I kill you. If you say da wrong shit outta your mouth, I kill you. If the pussy ain't what I think it is, I kill you. You have no win in this situation, but only you can determine if you want to live or die today."

Vivian understood every single word and nodded her head in agreement.

By the time I'm done with her fat ass, she gonna regret she gave birth to Willie, I thought. I cut her loose from the chair and had her lie on her back on top of a metal table. I grabbed her ankles and threw her legs over my shoulders. Her fat pussy popped up like a flat-screen TV. Without warning, I rammed my hammer into her until my balls were bouncing off her ass.

"God damn it! Dis pussy is hot!" I grunted. "Oh, God . . . Yeah . . . grab my dick with your pussy!" After twenty minutes of fucking Vivian and giving her wet pussy a black eye, I flipped her over on her stomach on the floor.

"Ooh! Ooh! Ooh! Ooh! It hurts! You hurting me!" Vivian felt her asshole being forced open.

"Bitch! Shut da fuck up! Before I kill you! Damn! Dis ass is good!"

Complying, Vivian lay still on the filthy floor, burying her face in a puddle of dirty water. I increased my speed. I fucked her asshole like a muthafucka coming home from prison after doing a twenty-year bid.

"You like it in da ass, don't you? I should make you lick my dick clean after I'm done. Oh shit! Aah." I placed one hand on the back of Vivian's neck and rammed her fast and hard until I felt my nut spitting out the tip of my dick. Releasing my nut felt like releasing a demon. Satisfied by the way I had torn Vivian a new asshole, I flipped her over on her back again and made her lick my dick and balls clean. Physically, Vivian was a hot mess. Psychologically, she was confused, because on one hand, she hated the fact that she had just been violated in the worst way, and on the other hand, never in her thirty-nine years had she been fucked in the ass the way I had put it on her.

Not seeing her feeling the pain I had inflicted on her had me pissed the fuck off. I wanted dis bitch to beg me for her life; instead, it appeared as if she was liking it. *Let's see if you gonna enjoy dis*, I thought to myself as I reached for my pants and pulled out a syringe I had laced up with heroin. Once I had Vivian tied up in the chair again, I stuck the syringe in her arm. Immediately the dope started taking control of her body. After vomiting and shitting on herself, she started nodding out. For ten days straight, I fed her dog food and a shot of Obsession three times a day. When I decided to cut her loose, the bitch couldn't even remember her name, or how she had ended up in the warehouse. She was a full-blown *tecata*, junkie, crawling, eating her own shit, and drinking her own urine.

"Yo, Ma! You are free to go," I told her, but she would respond by holding on to my leg like a child did to a mother or father.

"I don't wanna go! I need a shot of dope!"

"Oh, you don't wanna go! You want some more dope! Bitch, you got to earn dat!"

Vivian dropped to her knees and opened her mouth. I pulled out my dick and urinated in her mouth R. Kelly–style. I took pride in humiliating her. Once Miguelito had enough footage to make an hour-long DVD, I drove her down to Brook Avenue and dumped her ass out with the rest of the worthless whores.

Miguelito, being the computer whiz he was, uploaded the video from his phone to YouTube and also burned two thousand copies on a CD burner. These copies were given out for free all over the Bronx. Miguelito had made sure to blur our faces on the video. If we were rap artists looking for a come up, our video would've been platinum, because within twenty-four hours, niggas all over New York City were jonesing for a copy. The video was even covered by CNN and iReport.

Chapter Eight

You Can Run, but You Can't Hide

Miguelito

Three months later . . .

The weatherman's promise of a beautiful early summer day was fulfilled. Swimming pools around the city rushed to complete the necessary preparations to open their doors for the summer. At Crotona Park janitors were making their rounds of the facilities before the opening, and they stumbled upon a large package lying on the bottom of the swimming pool. They hauled the package out of the pool and discovered a body under all the duct tape and plastic.

"Normally, when I find 'em 'swimming,' the first thing I do is go through their pockets, take their jewelry if they got any, then call the police," said Poncho, a middle-aged Hispanic man, to his young partner, Alex, who was fresh out of high school and was working his first full-time summer job.

"I guess we don't need no medical examiner to tell us what we got here!" Alex said, smiling. Discovering a dead body was the norm for janitors in Crotona Park.

"We are shit out of luck! This one smells like hell! From the looks of things, this motherfucker been here awhile. I'm not touching this one. The stink won't wipe off easy." Poncho exhaled loudly as he stood inches away from the wrapped body, watching worms crawl around it. Realizing he had been holding his breath, he said to the rookie janitor, "Make the call, kid! We have to report this shit."

When the police arrived, they did their normal routine questioning. Then a fat slob with filthy nails took photographs of the crime scene. Afterward, a morgue attendant with a box cutter started cutting the duct tape off what was left of Tiffany. The plainclothes detectives were standing around laughing, looking like unwanted guests at a party. The two morgue attendants rolled the corpse like a piece of trash onto a body bag, then threw the bag on top of a canvas stretcher.

***

The Sugar Shack Club down in Hunts Point was packed. Reggaeton music blared out of the speakers as a a short, hot Puerto Rican girl worked the pussy pole. The air in the club smelled like fast food, weed, hard-core liquor, and sweaty pussy. Within the darkness of the club, a Philly blunt was lit and a private lap dance was in session.

High rollers and corner boys were stuffing their dirty money in between the luscious ass cheeks of some dark-skinned chick who was bent down on the stage, giving everyone a view of her pink, hairless slit.

At the other side of the bar, Willie was sitting down, drinking and contemplating his next move, oblivious to the five niggas who were watching him. He counted the small wad of cash. It had been a rough night. He had made the rounds and still hadn't come up with a vic to rob. Drug dealers in all five boroughs were hunting for his head. The nigga was worth more dead than alive. Seventy-five thousand dollars in cash, no questions asked. Ever since he had robbed Tungo, Miguelito, and Grip, Willie's heart had been pumping mad shit. Unbeknownst to him, Tungo and his young goons were closing the distance between them, and they had a surprise for him.

"Care for another drink, nigga?" said a low voice.

Willie sprang to attention. He looked into the eyes of a young assassin. One of same young niggas he had ripped off for a brick of heroin.

"Nah! I'm not drinking. What's up?"

"You're a smart man, so I don't have to tell you what you're heading for, do I? I don't want to body your ass. If I did, you would've been dead a long time ago. Dis doesn't mean I won't air you the fuck out right here. Now, get da fuck up and let's take a walk. I want to show you something! I want you to see what your grimy ass created."

"If y'all gonna kill me, do it now, niggas!"

"I already told you, I'm not gonna kill you. I just want you to see what you created," Tungo responded.

Willie was intimidated, afraid to die. He moved slowly, his body tense.

Once he and Tungo were outside, Willie was manhandled into the back seat of a stolen SUV and driven down to Brook Avenue.

"When was the last time you seen your motha or wifey?" Grip said as he pressed the PLAY button on the DVD player on the back seat of the SUV. When an image popped up on the TV screen, Willie's eyes got watery.

"Damn! My baby mom and my mom had nothing to do with us! Y'all niggas are out of pocket."

"You're wrong, my nigga! You see, you created dis shit! Look at your bitch getting her ass whipped.

Just wait till you see your mom taking it up da ass! Nigga, dat brick you stole from us ain't shit compared to what we did to your mom!" Tungo replied.

When the DVD reached the part where Willie's mother was getting her asshole busted open, Tungo pressed the PAUSE button. Noticing the hateful gleam in Willie's eyes, Tungo decided to inflict more mental pain.

"What kind of nigga will subject his motha to dat kind of treatment? You see, you fucked around with da wrong young niggas. However, I do got a li'l compassion in my heart, so I'ma take you to see your mom. I'm sure she's worried about you."

After forcing Willie to watch the entire DVD, Tungo and Grip dropped him off on the corner of Beekman Avenue, where Vivian had spent the last three months turning tricks and shooting up dope.

The dirty-looking Latina heroin addict looked up at her son fearfully. Her right eye was completely shut from an ass whipping Miguelito had put on her ass earlier that day. Her clothes were tattered. She was barefoot, and scratches and scabs covered her entire body.

"My God, Mom! What them niggas done to you?" Willie repeated softly as he reached out to hug his mother. She flinched and ran her tongue over the nasty deep cut on her upper lip.

"I suck your dick if you buy me a bag of dope, please!"

"No!" Willie knelt down in front of his mother and cried in earnest, "I'm sorry, Mom! I swear, I'm gonna kill them niggas."

Vivian nodded, then yelled, "Leave me alone! Leave me alone!"

Tungo pressed the gas pedal to the floor, and the SUV leaped forward at full speed and crashed into Willie and Vivian. The SUV hit them with such a force that Vivian was stuck underneath the truck. After throwing the truck in reverse, Tungo ran over Willie's motionless body, which was lying in the middle of the street. When he stomped on the gas pedal again, the SUV lunged forward, then disappeared into the night.

Chapter Nine

The Wild Cowboys

Rashad

The public murder of Willie and his mother delivered a clear message to the streets that the Pop Rulers were not to be fucked with. Anyone who dared to test our gangsta would suffer a bloodthirsty affair.

The streets of the Boogie Down Bronx were blazing with our names, and the media branded us with the nickname the Wild Cowboys Jr., after the notorious Dominican gang that had rained terror down on the Bronx in the late eighties and early nineties. We felt offended by that name. The difference between them and us was that we, the Pop Rulers, killed only muthafuckas who deserved to be killed.

Our turf encompassed an area that stretched between Mott Haven, Brook Avenue, Cypress Avenue, 141st Street, Willis Avenue, Beekman Avenue, 149th and Prospect Avenue, Union Street, Beck Street, and Fox Street. Plus, we didn't allow Dominicans to be part of our crew. We had let it be known that we were not allowing them to get money on our turf. We had no problem airing a *platano*, a banana-eating Dominican, the fuck out. The original Wild Cowboys were a bunch of snitches who had flipped on each other like politicians did once shit got hot in their camp. So to name us after a bunch of rats was like a slap to our faces. Shit was about to get ugly.

Orchard Beach, Section Four . . .

July 4, 2002, promised to be a good day. Section Four at Orchard Beach was bumping as reggaeton music dominated the airwaves. Chicks in all shapes and sizes were parading in their bikinis, showing off their asses and tits.

Puerto Ricans, Blacks, Dominicans, Cubans, and *gringas* (white girls) were all congregating with ballas, crab niggas, hot niggas, fag niggas, and wannabe thugged-out niggas, in hopes of locking themselves down a nice nigga.

Orchard Beach, Section Four, was where niggas from the other four boroughs came to show off their latest grown men's toys: bikes and cars. It was where record companies came to introduce their new talent. In the winter months, Orchard Beach served as a dumping ground for niggas who weren't cut out to serve in the war in the Boogie Down Bronx.

As the sun beamed down on the half-naked bitches, Miguelito, Dirty D, Tungo, Fatima, and I chilled out by the handball court, where a reggaeton artist from Puerto Rico named Don Omar was getting ready to rock the mic. The crowd was hyped up by DJ Enuff. Bodies were shaking against each other. Bikinis and thongs were being pushed to the side, and young niggas were getting their freak on. Clouds of smoke from lit blunts were up in the air. Muthafuckas were celebrating Independence Day without a care in the world.

Out of the corner of my eye, I observed four pretty niggas mean mugging us a little too hard. It was obvious that two of them were twins. "Ay, yo! Do any of y'all know them niggas over there, looking at us hard and shit?" I asked, pointing at the four young niggas, who were now walking in our direction.

"Nah. They're probably some stickup niggas looking for a quick come up. Let's see what they want," Miguelito responded and immediately patted his waist to remind himself that he had his burner with him.

"Yo, what's up? Ain't y'all niggas the Wild Cowboys from down the BX?" one of the twins asked Miguelito. He was looking at Miguelito as if he was trying to remember him from somewhere.

"Nah. We're from Brooklyn," Grip responded as one of the young niggas put his hand at his waist.

Pop! Pop! Pop! Pop! Pop!

Shots rang out, and all four pretty niggas hit the beach's hot-ass sand in slow motion, choking on their own blood.

Everyone ran out of the handball court and raced to their cars and bikes in the parking lot.

"Them niggas are dead! They got shot in the face! Look at the holes in their grills!" said one bystander as he stepped over one of the twins while making his way out of the handball court.

"Are they still breathing?" asked another bystander.

The beach police and an ambulance pulled up to the handball court, and immediately the police and the paramedics placed the four young bucks onto stretchers and rushed them to Jacobi Hospital.

"Yo! What da fuck happened back there?" I asked Miguelito about an hour later, after we sat down to eat shrimp and lobster tails at a restaurant down on City Island.

"I don't know, and I don't care! Dat nigga was reaching for his burner, so I burned him first. Fuck 'em! They shouldn't be frontin' like they were gangstas and shit," he responded while focusing on the plate of shrimp in front of him.

The next day, the *New York Times* and Fox News reported the quadruple shooting in Orchard Beach. One of the headlines on the front page of the *Times* read BRONX DISTRICT ATTORNEY'S TWIN SONS SHOT TO DEATH IN ORCHARD BEACH. I scanned the article.

Yesterday, at approximately 1:30 p.m., the Bronx district attorney's twin sons and two of their friends were shot dead in Orchard Beach. Bronx DA Jimmy Wise identified his twin sons, Ruben and Robe Wise, at Jacobi Hospital. The two other victims are awaiting identification by a family member.

The police have no suspects, no witnesses have come forward, and there is no motive for this public execution of four innocent young men. Police are still questioning people who were at the beach at the time of the shooting and are searching for clues.

Reggaeton artist Don Omar is offering to pay for the funerals of the four young men. A five-thousand-dollar reward is being offered for any information that leads to the arrest and conviction of any suspects. . . .

The case became a priority and remained so for two weeks. Detectives swarmed the streets, looking for any clues. They asked everyone about the murders: young people, old people, men and women. It didn't matter. If you were breathing, you were getting asked about the murders. No one said anything.

The case was eventually logged as unsolved and transferred down to the NYPD's homicide investigating unit, or HIU, which specialized in cracking difficult murder cases in New York City.

Chapter Ten

The Badlands

La Puta

July 6, 2002 . . .

"Listen to me, Rashad. I know what I'm doing. Trust me. When I get down to Philly, I will give you a call. Right now, I'm being told by the Colombians that we could double our money down there. I'ma also look at a few locations to open up a few strip clubs while I'm down there."

"Mom, you don't even know those Colombians! How do you know dis is not a setup? Plus, I don't trust dat punk boy Flash or his bitch-ass father. You know they blame—"

"I'm not stupid, baby. Flash's father is trying to hustle me, too, for money for a sex change operation. The way I see it, if his punk ass wants

some money, he's gonna have to earn every penny
I give him. I'm gonna use his ass until I familiarize
myself with the city. If he acts stupid, I'll body his
ass," La Puta said as she pulled a 9 mm out of her
Gucci bag.

"Damn, Mom! Where da fuck did you get dat
from?"

"You know Mom's got to keep a li'l protection.
You never know when one of those fools out there
are gonna act up."

"I feel you, Mom. I'm just glad I'm your son!"

"I'm leaving in about an hour, so I'm gonna need
you to let me hold twenty-one bricks. You know
the deal. Fifty-fifty."

"You're late! I already got them stashed in the
violet-blue Mercedes-Maybach. You already know
how to get into the stash, right?"

"Yeah."

"Mom, I'm gonna have some associates down in
Philly look out for you. I don't think you should be
rolling around there by yourself. Niggas in Philly
are dirty."

"I'm a big girl, Rashad."

"I know, Mom. But we both know dis game don't
respect no one."

"Who da fuck you know down in Philly?"

"I've got a few close associates who cop dope
from me. One of them runs a crew of young goons
known as the Puerto Rican Mafia, P.R.M. They got
Philly on smash."

"A'ight. It don't hurt to have a li'l protection."

"I got your back, Mom."

"I know you do, baby."

Fifth Street and Annsbury Street, North Philadelphia . . .

I pulled up in front of Tierra Colombiana Restaurant and Nightclub in my violet-blue Mercedes-Maybach with scissor doors, stopping traffic and letting niggas and bitches know that a new queen bee had just arrived in town, and her name was La Puta. I was immediately greeted by Crazy Horse, otherwise known as *el jefe de los maleantes*, the boss of all the thugs. He was the head nigga in charge of the infamous Puerto Rican Mafia, which specialized in the dope game. When he said, "Jump," the only thing niggas would ask was, "How high?"

"Damn! My man Rashad never told me his mother was this gorgeous!" Crazy Horse said as soon as I stepped out of my ride.

His gaze moved down to my pussy. I smiled, because I knew my Baby Phat jeans were hugging my fat pussy like a boxing glove. "Listen. I got to go up in dat spot and see a few of my associates. Afterward, you could drive me around. I need to make a few stops, and I need to find a spot to lay my head."

Damn, Ma! You could stay with me! Rashad's my man and all, but I got to hit that pussy! Crazy Horse thought. "That's what I'm here for. I gave my man Rashad my word that I would keep you safe."

Nigga, please! I see da way you're staring at my pussy. You are one ugly muthafucka, but I'm willing to bet you got a big dick! Damn! Where da fuck you get a nose dat big? I thought to myself as we walked into Tierra Colombiana. If I didn't know better, I could swear that he was related to KRS-One. His eyes were wide, and his mouth was crooked. I seen some ugly niggas in my life, but dis clown took da crown of the ugliest nigga in the dope game!

To my surprise, a familiar face from da Bronx was up in the house tonight, performing his new hit single "Lean Back." When he saw my face, his whole demeanor changed. I acted like I didn't see him, but he made it his business to come over to the table I was sitting at and run his fucking mouth. But before he got close to the table, Crazy Horse was on his feet, ready to smash him.

"I just came to say hi to an old friend," he told Crazy Horse in a low tone of voice.

Crazy Horse kept his eyes on him as his hand traveled down to his waist.

"Congratulations on your new hit song! You're still wack!" I said with a smile when he stepped closer.

"Fuck outta my face, groupie!"

"Nigga, don't ever get slick at the mouth with me! We both know you're pure pussy! Do I need to remind you what my son did to you?" I replied.

"Hold! Hold! Hold! What's going on here?" asked a well-dressed Colombian man.

"Nothing. Just a groupie acting up," Joey Wack said in a hostile voice.

"Nigga, let that be the last time you disrespect my people!" Crazy Horse said, ready to bang Joey Wack's head off his shoulders.

"Fuck you, nigga! I'm the star in this house!" Joey Wack said while looking at his entourage for moral support.

"Big man! You and your little entourage can bounce!" said the Colombian capo, whom everyone called Capo. He was protecting his interests.

"Nigga, we'll bounce after you cough up thirty thousand for my performance!" Joey said, feeling himself.

"Y'all Bronx niggas are about to be sent back to New York in body bags if y'all don't bounce!" Capo signaled to five of his young goons who served as security in the place and who were willing to make their presence known.

"Capo, you gonna burn me for my money over a bitch you don't even know? I know this bitch! She's dirty! The bitch got no love for no one!" Joey Wack said.

But Capo wasn't trying to hear that shit. His mind was on what I was bringing to the table: twenty-one kilos of pure African dope.

"Nigga, you heard him! Bounce, before I make it rain up in dis bitch! You fat, nasty pig! Lean back on dat!" I said as I pulled my 9 mm out of my Gucci bag and aimed it at Joey Wack's head.

Damn! This bitch is out of her mind! What the fuck! I hope she don't shoot this nigga up in my club. I don't need the drama. I got to holla at Rashad first chance I get, Capo thought. "*Espera un momentito!* Wait a minute, baby girl! I don't need this mess up in my club. Put that gun back in your bag before shit gets ugly," Capo said, trying to avoid a sticky situation popping off.

"You're right, *papi*. Dis nigga gets to live one more day, based on you," I said and blew a kiss to Joey Wack.

"I'll see you in court, Capo!" Joey said as he was walking out of the door.

"Nigga, stay away from Philly! If I ever see any of y'all clowns in my part of town, believe me, y'all will be heading back to New York in body bags!" Capo said, mean mugging him.

One hour later . . .

Crazy Horse and I were up in Pizza Fina, a pizzeria on Fifth and Luray that was used as a stash spot for the Colombians in North Philly. The back room was used to cut up 90 percent of the dope in Philadelphia.

Three heavily armed bodyguards stood at their posts while four naked hood rats were bagging up dope. I was impressed with the operation that Capo was running. Morphine, B_{12}, quaaludes, and four cases of glassine bags sat on a glass table next to a fish tank. Two sterling silver McDonald's spoons were on top of the one brick I had given to Capo. The room looked like a candy shop.

"*Mami chula*, here you go. You got to put this mask and these latex gloves on if you're gonna be around this shit. If the smell starts to get to you, drink some milk and eat some of those crackers over there. That will settle your stomach," Capo said, pointing to a small table.

The nigga was lecturing me, as if I was new to da dope game. I must admit, he was one of the best dope cutters on the East Coast, though. "Tell me something, Capo. How much cut do one of these babies hold?" I asked him while holding the brick of dope in my hand. I pretty much had an idea, but I wanted to learn the way da Colombians cut their dope.

"Being as though it's pure African dope, I believe it can stand a fifteen. But I'ma only put ten, so we can get rid of it quick."

"How fast can we get rid of dis shit?"

"One day, at the most."

"Really?"

"Baby, Philly is a dope heaven! That bitch Fefa La Dominicana is going to be mad. Once y'all put that shit on the streets, her business will go down, trust me," Crazy Horse said.

I wanted to believe him, because I knew my shit was tight, but I had a gut feeling about him. Something about him wasn't right. *Bitch, stop tripping!* da li'l diva in my head was telling me.

"Capo, I got twenty-one bricks available," I said. "If you're only gonna put a ten, that means these twenty-one bricks will convert themselves into two hundred and ten bricks. Let's bag up dis one brick first and see how dat does. If I'm correct, one brick holding a ten adds up to eight thousand. If we bag it up in twenty-dollar bags, dat will be eighty thousand bags, with a net profit of one-point-six million dollars. I don't think da streets of Philly are ready for dis shit. Let's get dat chicken money together!" I was letting the Colombians know that I was sharp with my math, in case they had any funny ideas.

"You want to see how good this shit is?" Capo asked me with a smile.

"Sure!" I responded.

He unzipped his pants and pulled out his small dick and poured a li'l bit of dope on the head, then ordered one of the girls who were bagging to suck his dick. "Come here, China. Suck this dope dick for *papi*."

The dope was so strong that as China began to suck him off, she started convulsing. White foam dripped from her mouth, and her eyes rolled to the back of her head.

Capo gripped her by her hair and threw her on the floor and turned toward me. "You see that shit! The bitch couldn't even handle a match head! Just imagine what a bag would do!"

I was speechless. The other three girls glanced over at us in disbelief, unable to save their friend, who had overdosed on some dope dick.

After we were done bagging up the eighty thousand bags, Capo's team hit the streets of Philadelphia with one mission in mind: money, power, and respect!

"Listen, Capo. I will check in with you tomorrow night. Right now, I got a few people I must see before I call it a night." I looked at Crazy Horse and asked, "Do you know how to get to Fifth and Cambria Street? I need to see my youngest son."

"Yeah. That's only five minutes from here."

"Good. Let's go," I said, handing him my car keys.

Five minutes later . . .

The residence in which Flash and his father lived was located on a block heavily populated by junkies. Broken-down cars littered half of the block.

As soon as Crazy Horse and I stepped inside the house, I pulled out my cell phone and tweeted Rashad a short message.

"Mom, are you staying with us?" Flash asked me while looking Crazy Horse up and down.

"Baby, I would love to, but I got too much class to lay my ass down in this roach-infested place!"

"What? You too good for us, huh? You forgot where you came from, huh?" my son's father shouted as he walked toward me from the other side of the living room.

"Call it what you want to call it!" I barked.

"Fuck you!" my son's father yelled in my face.

I wanted to smack the bitch out of him, but I decided to give him a pass. "Fuck me, huh? Nigga, fucking me is something your bitch ass couldn't do right! You nasty-ass punk!" I said in a calm voice, smiling.

"Whatever!" he responded.

I turned to my son. "Flash, I'll be around tomorrow. Make sure you're ready to go at one p.m. I'm gonna take your ass shopping."

"Fuck you, Mom! You don't have to do shit for me! You ain't never done shit for me anyway."

"Have it your way!" I said and walked out of the house. I really wasn't trying to hear my faggot son run his mouth, taking up for his daddy.

Once back in my car, I reached into my bag and pulled out a wad of cash. I peeled off five thousand dollars and handed it to Crazy Horse. "Listen. I appreciate everything you've done. If you want to keep me company tomorrow, I'll be glad to roll with you."

"Fuck tomorrow! I wanna keep you company tonight!"

"Let me see your dick, nigga!" My jaw dropped when the ugly nigga pulled out his dick.

"Eleven and a half inches. That's why they call me Crazy Horse! Do you like what you see?" he teased.

I bent my head down and deep throated him with one motion. I flexed my throat a li'l, which drove him crazy. I wanted him to know that I was not a punk bitch. I massaged the perineum—the area between the balls and his ass—with my fingers. I rotated my head. I had him squirming and moaning. I looked up at him and winked. I felt the head of his dick swell in my mouth, and I knew he was about to come. I tightened my lips and swallowed his man juice. I loved the power I felt when I was sucking a nigga off. But I couldn't explain the mixed feelings I had about sucking this ugly nigga off. On one hand, I was horny, much hornier than I had realized, until I finished swallowing his cum. "I hope you can fuck!" I said as we drove away.

Twenty minutes later, we had a room at a Marriott Hotel. Once inside the cozy room, I wasted no time in taking control.

"Nigga, I want to fuck!" I said and grabbed his dick.

"Suck me again?" he asked while shaking his swollen purple dick head at me.

"I'm calling the shots here, and I say I want some dick!"

"How do you want it?"

"Standing up against the wall."

He grabbed me and threw my ass against the wall and unceremoniously shoved his dick up my pussy.

"Give it to me hard and fast! I want to feel your balls banging against my ass!"

"Damn!"

This ugly nigga was plowing into my pussy so hard that he almost lifted me up off the floor. I couldn't get enough of his dick. Ordinarily I would try to satisfy the nigga I was with, but today was all about me.

"I'm cumming!" I yelled. I grunted loudly as I squeezed his dick with my pussy lips. Once I was done cumming, I pushed him off me.

"You bitch!" he snarled. "I haven't come yet!"

"Dat's your problem! Now, get da fuck out of my room before I call security on you!" I said.

"It's all good, baby!"

"It better be! Now, get da fuck out!"

Once Crazy Horse was out of my room, I took a shower, got dressed, then walked down to the reception desk and changed rooms.

Chapter Eleven

Busted

La Puta

Early the next morning, I awoke with a smirk on my face. I was still feeling the effects of Crazy Horse's dick. My pussy was calling for more dick. *Maybe tonight I'll let dat ugly nigga tear me a new asshole!* I thought to myself as I prepared to meet up with Capo.

I was surprised to hear on every news channel in Philadelphia reports of the huge number of dope fiends being rushed to local hospitals after overdosing on killer dope. In the dope game, when people overdosed, it could only mean one thing: money, money, money, and more money! Every dope fiend in the city wanted to get a taste of the killer dope that was sending muthafuckas to emergency rooms all over the city.

As I stood outside the Marriott Hotel, I heard footsteps and then I saw a few white men rushing past me. I made my way toward my car, only to see a black SUV with smoked windows double-parked beside me, blocking my way. *Damn! Now I gotta wait for dis asshole to move! Some muthafuckas don't understand dat time is money in my world*, I grumbled silently. I walked around the SUV to see if there was anyone inside, but I was stopped in my tracks when I saw the same two white men who'd just rushed past me heading in my direction.

"Vicky 'La Puta' Lopez, freeze! This is the FBI!" one of them shouted.

I reached into my Gucci bag and gripped my 9 mm. *I'm not going down without a fight! They're gonna have to kill me if they want me!* I slowly pulled my hand out of my bag and aimed for one of the white men's head. In slow, surrealistic motion, I pulled the trigger and hit my target right between the eyes.

"Take that bitch down! Take her down!" the other FBI agent yelled as he rendered assistance to his partner. Suddenly, four more agents swarmed the area around my car and the SUV.

Shit! I'm hit! I thought to myself as I looked at my lower left leg, which was barely attached to my kneecap. I lay next to my car, soaking wet with blood and numb. I tried to get up, but my body wouldn't respond.

"Is she dead?" I heard one of the agents say as they approached me from both sides of the car.

"Bitch, if you even blink, I will put a bullet hole in your head! Blink, bitch!" another agent shouted at me.

Through my blurred vision I managed to look over at the FBI agent that I had shot, and the only thing I saw was a chunk of his face lying on the sidewalk and brain matter spewing out of his head. Crimson blood decorated the sidewalk. At that moment, I knew I was done.

Damn! I got caught slipping! I should've listened to Rashad! I thought to myself right before I lost consciousness.

That same day, Hahnemann University Hospital . . .

I awoke and found myself handcuffed to a bed, heavily medicated, with IVs in my arms, plastic tubes in my nose and mouth, and my left leg missing from the knee down. I wanted to scream, but the tubes in my mouth wouldn't let me. I tried to pull the IVs out of my arms, but I couldn't. Both of my arms were cuffed to the bed.

"The bitch is awake," a female agent said as she approached my bed.

"Ms. Lopez, we're glad you made it," she said as she pulled her gun from her holster and began hitting me on my bandaged leg, where it had been amputated. The pain was beyond anything I had ever experienced in my life.

She glared down at me and said in a monotone, "Vicky Lopez, you are under arrest for the murder of Federal Agent Jermaine Willsky, for conspiracy to transport a controlled substance, and for money laundering. Do you understand your rights?"

I just looked at this bitch with a smirk. There was nothing they could do to me that would make me want to talk.

The FBI agent leaned forward until she had her mouth close to my ear, then said, "It's not over yet. You dirty-ass Puerto Rican whore, you killed my brother! I will see to it that you get the death penalty!" And then she hit me one more time with her gun.

The other FBI agent on duty watched, with a smile on his face.

Rashad

The South Bronx . . .

My cell phone rang as I walked into my apartment after a night of partying. I checked the number and didn't recognize it, but I answered it anyway.

"Hello, Rashad." The voice sounded low.

"Who da fuck is dis?"

"Rashad, it's me, Crazy Horse, from down in Philly. I'm calling you because something bad just went down with your mom."

"Nigga, stop playing with me! I'm not in the mood for jokes!"

"For real, my nigga. Your mom was busted and shot up by the Feds this morning. They got her under watch in the hospital. I don't have any details, but it don't look good. Word is, she killed an FBI agent."

I was shocked to hear that La Puta had killed an FBI agent. This shit was serious. I felt the tears rolling down my face. The last time I had cried was when my grandfather got murdered. "Not my mother!" I yelled and dropped to the floor.

"Rashad! Rashad! Listen to me! Get your ass down here today! I believe they're gonna try to arraign her tomorrow morning. The Feds are all over this case."

"Big homie, have you tried to get in contact with my li'l brother, Flash?"

"My nigga, I'ma keep one hundred with you. Your li'l brother is the reason your mom got popped!"

"What—" I began to say, but Crazy Horse cut me off.

"Your li'l brother and his father got busted last night, while trying to sell a pound of weed to an undercover federal agent, and decided to drop a dime on your mom."

"You sure? How do you know dis?"

"Nigga, my sister is a detective down here, and she gave me a copy of the arrest warrant and police report."

"I'll be down in a few hours!"

"One more thing, my nigga. Your mom lost one of her legs in the shoot-out!" Crazy Horse said before hanging up the phone.

I sat on the floor with the dead phone pressed against my ear, trying to think. After a while, I put the phone in my pocket and stormed out of my apartment. I drove to Prospect Avenue, in search of my nigga Miguelito, who was known for hanging out on the block. He spotted my car the second I turned onto Union Street.

"Nigga, why you look so nervous?" he asked me as he jumped into the front seat of my car.

"Yo, B! La Puta got shot up and arrested by the Feds down in Philly!"

"Nigga, stop playing!"

"Do I look like I'm playing?"

The silence that followed was broken when Miguelito said, "Are you all right? I'm here for you, my nigga."

"I got to take a ride down to Philly. I'ma need you to handle business for me up here."

Miguelito took a moment to reply. "I want to go with you. We are family."

"Nah. I'm taking Dirty D and Fatima with me. I don't know what's happening, but I do know one thing. I'm gonna kill my brother, feel me? So, one of us gotta stay here and hold shit down. I trust you."

"I got your back, B," Miguelito said with a frown on his face.

"Da situation is serious! Putting a Band-Aid on dis ain't gonna work. So, if I don't come back, you and Fatima will be in charge. My nigga, I gotta go." I gave Miguelito a brotherly hug and the keys to my apartment and the stash houses.

He got out of my car, and I drove off with hate in my heart.

La Puta

FBI headquarters, Downtown Philadelphia . . .

I was thrown into a wheelchair, cuffed to it, and taken down to FBI headquarters right from the hospital. *I can't believe this shit is going down like this*! I thought as I was paraded in front of the FBI building for the media.

"The *Philadelphia Daily News* is going to run a story tonight in a special edition about how a no-good drug-runner bitch killed an FBI agent! If you deny a single word, I will kill you myself! Try me if you want!" a white FBI agent said angrily.

"Ms. Lopez, are you guilty?" a CNN reporter yelled.

"The FBI is trying to kill me!" I yelled back at the reporter, only to be rushed into the building.

"Ms. Lopez, let me give it to you raw. You're going down! I will see to it that you receive the death penalty!" the white agent growled once we were alone inside an interrogation room.

"Me no speak no *inglés*!" I replied with a smirk.

"Maybe you understand this! Two-forty-one, S.C.S. section eight-fourteen, prohibited act—intent to distribute a controlled substance. In your case, twenty kilos of heroin. Let me make it plain and simple for you. You're going to rot in jail, *comprende*? Understand that?"

"Fuck you!"

"Mm-hmm!" the white agent answered as he sat down on the edge of the rectangular table that occupied a large part of the room.

"I want a lawyer!" I said.

"You're going to need more than a lawyer! Firearms penalties, one-eighty-four S.C.S., section nine-twenty-four C-one states that you are a perfect candidate. You see, Ms. Lopez, in addition to the twenty kilos of heroin in the trunk of your car, we found a short-barrel rifle, a shotgun, and a semiautomatic assault weapon. For each weapon, it's ten years. And we also found a machine gun and three silencers. In case you didn't know, the machine gun alone carries thirty years. Lastly, murder one! You still want to play dumb?"

"Fuck outta my face, cracka!"

"Since you are the hottest chick on the block, the principal administrator, the head bitch in charge, we're going to charge you with the RICO Act. *Comprende* that?" The FBI agent sounded annoyed. He had taken my answers as a professional insult.

Finally, I was putting my street legal education to good use. "Whatever!"

"There are going to be a lot of lonely nights for you," another FBI agent said. He had just joined us in the interrogation room.

"I believe the FBI will be missing one of its members! His family is going to suffer a lot of lonely nights also!" I retorted.

"Very funny, Ms. Lopez!" said the second agent.

"Okay! You convinced me, all right? I'll tell you everything I know, but I want a deal!" I said with a smile.

"Ms. Lopez, you killed a federal agent. The only thing we can promise you at this time is that we will inform the judge that you cooperated with us," said the second agent as he pulled out a chair and sat right in front of me, fixing his blue eyes on me. He must have thought he had broken me, because he took his black tie off and placed a mini tape recorder on top of the table.

I remained silent.

"Ms. Lopez, whenever you're ready," the first agent said.

I looked at him and gathered the biggest ball of spit in my mouth and spit in his face. Then I yelled, "Y'all faggot FBI could throw the whole book of law at me, and I still won't break! Y'all could shoot both of my legs off ,and I still would say, 'Fuck y'all!' I'm not a soft bitch. I'm a hard bitch with more balls than y'all muthafuckas! I don't give a fuck about life anymore! Fuck da FBI and the RICO Act! I'm Vicky Lopez from da Bronx, muthafuckas!" My adrenaline was in overdrive.

"Bitch, you're going to have your day in court!" the first FBI agent said calmly, wiping the spit from his eyes. Then he pushed me and the wheel-chair into the wall.

Flash Lopez

The federal detention center in Philadelphia . . .

I sat across from two agents in a secluded room in the federal detention center, scared to death. I was with my father when we were arrested while trying to sell a pound of weed to an undercover federal agent. For some reason, this agent seemed to believe that I was the one who had approached him, so they'd given me the case. My father had been cut loose after three hours of questioning, and I'd been detained.

"Mr. Lopez, by now you understand the severity of your situation. You are looking at a long time in prison. You're young, and you've got your entire life ahead of you. I think you're a good kid, so I want to help you get past this. I might be able to get your case thrown out, but you need to help me. Give me information that I can use to catch the real drug dealers you know," said one of the agents sitting across from me.

I didn't hesitate. "My mother. She is here with a bunch of heroin. She works for my brother. You find her, and you've got a newsworthy bust. She's driving around in a blue Mercedes-Maybach. I bet she's staying at a Marriott. She loves them hotels."

"What's her name?"

"Vicky. Vicky Lopez. She goes by the name La Puta."

The agent who had spoken gave his partner a look. "Check that name in the computer."

The partner quickly left the interrogation room.

When he returned, I told the Feds everything they wanted to know in less than fifteen minutes.

In exchange, they assured me that we had a deal and that I would be free to go that very day.

Many of you would classify me as a snitch, but I really don't give a fuck, because it was either snitch hard and go home or keep my lips sealed and do some time. I'll be honest. I was not built to be sitting in jail. Plus, my mom had never really done shit for me. Snitching on her was the easiest thing I'd ever done in my life.

Another agent entered the room. He was tall, square jawed, and muscular. He sat across from me. "Mr. Lopez, my name is Agent Thomas Loukiski, and I'm here to inform you of our previous deal. You help us, we help you."

"I already told you everything I know!"

"We appreciate your assistance thus far. But we need you to agree to testify against your mother, Vicky Lopez. We will hold you until the trial is over," Agent Loukiski said as he reached up and rubbed his forehead.

"That wasn't part of our deal!"

"Son, shit happens!"

"If I refuse, what will happen?"

"You will go to prison, and I will charge you with everything I can think of." Agent Loukiski then rose from his chair and walked out of the room.

Twenty minutes later, he returned, with a stern look on his face. "What's it going to be, Mr. Lopez? I don't have all day. I've got a funeral to attend."

"I want to do my time until the trial in a country-club prison. I don't want to be in the company of murderers and drug dealers. I'll testify if you can assure me that I won't do no more than a year in prison," I said with feeling.

"Mr. Lopez, I can assure you that you will be well taken care of. Once you testify, you will be let out of prison with a new identity, and we'll relocate you and your father. The Feds have a lot of resources available."

"I hear you loud and clear! I'm in! I will testify against my mother. I'll do it." I knew enough information that I could write a book on the topic, and I was gonna use that information to get myself off the loop.

Rashad

North Philly, that same night . . .

It was a quarter past twelve midnight when Fatima, Dirty D, and I arrived in North Philly. I parked in front of Crazy Horse's house on Third and Indiana. After checking out the block for a while, I took out my cell phone and dialed his number.

"Speak!" a female voice said.

"Is Crazy Horse there?"

"Wait a fucking minute!" the female said.

After too long, in my opinion, a male voice came on the line. "Yo, who the fuck is dis?"

"It's me, Rashad. I'm outside your crib."

"I'll be there in a second." Crazy Horse walked out of his house with his cell phone still pressed to his ear. He looked around, trying to locate me. I observed him for a moment. The block was clear of pedestrians. Once I felt safe, I blew the horn, and he walked over and jumped in the back seat with Dirty D.

"My nigga! I'm happy to see you, and—" he began, but I cut him off.

"Yo, B, I'm glad to see you too, but I need to know what's popping with my mom."

"Yo, shit don't look good. Your mom shot and killed an FBI agent. They found twenty kilos of dope and a whole bunch of weapons in the trunk of her car. On top of all that, your li'l brother is the main witness against her."

"Are you sure?"

"Yo, my people is a detective, and she managed to give me a copy of his arrest warrant and the statement he made to the FBI."

Crazy Horse reached into his back pocket and pulled out three pieces of folded paper and handed them to me. After I read them, I was filled with rage. I wanted to kill my brother and anybody associated with him. "I can't believe dis!"

"My nigga, the streets are hot right now. But I do have another surprise for you. I know where your brother's father is staying. I will drive you around there, but I will not participate in anything else."

"Yo, B, you done more than enough. I'll make sure I repay you double. What about my brother? Do you know where he is or where they got him?"

"My people informed me they're holding him at the federal detention center, in PC, protective custody. I believe he'll be transferred to Heavenford Prison until your mom goes to court."

"Yo, just show me where his father is staying!"

Ten minutes later . . .

Doña Lola, the woman who had made the mistake of giving birth to Flash Santiago, knew nothing of her faggot son's business. All she knew about her son was that he had relocated to Philadelphia with his son and had come out of the closet. She lived happily until she was awakened by a blow to the side of her head. A gut feeling told her that something was wrong, but she managed to say, "Take all the money!"

"Where is your son, Flash?" Fatima asked her.

"He's sleeping in the basement!" she responded with fear in her eyes.

"If dis old bag of shit moves, shoot her in da head!" I instructed Fatima before Dirty D and I made our way to the basement of the house.

Seconds later, I was standing over two naked, bitch-ass faggots who were laid out on a mattress. "Yo, shoot the punk bitch on the left!" I said, trying to keep my voice under control.

Dirty D lifted his 9 mm with the silencer and pulled the trigger. The bullet caught the punk bitch in the jugular vein, and immediately, blood started pumping out of his neck. For insurance, Dirty D put two more bullets into his head.

Flash's father tossed and turned and sat up in bed with his eyes half closed.

"Open your eyes, faggot!" I whispered and smacked him in the mouth with my hand.

"What! What is this?" Flash asked, trying to figure out what was transpiring.

"What does it look like? Get da fuck up and keep your dick-sucking mouth shut!" I roared.

Once I had Flash and his mother in the living room, I looked at Dirty D and Fatima. No dialogue was needed for them to know what was about to take place.

"Li'l man, I'm sorry to hear about your mother. I'm sure she'll be all right," Flash said while trying to cover his dick and hide it from his mother.

"Dis is not about my mother. Dis is about you and my brother setting her up! It's time to pay!" I gripped his mother by the neck and placed my 9 mm to her head.

"Stop!" Flash managed to yell like a bitch.

"Stop? Nigga, dis is not a game!" I responded. Before Flash could say another word, I squeezed the trigger and pumped two bullets into his mother's head. I pushed Doña Lola onto the floor, and a cry of pain escaped her mouth.

There was nothing Flash could do. His mother died with her eyes open. Tears blinded him. He couldn't accept that I had shot his mother in front of him. "Why, man? Why my mother?"

"Pussy, I should be asking you da same!" I yelled.

Flash knelt down next to his mother. I stood over him. The shot blew the back of his head off. He didn't resemble anything pleasurable to look at.

Flash's and Doña Lola's deaths made the front page of the "ghetto news," but they garnered only a small paragraph in the city's *Daily News*.

Two weeks later . . .

Fatima retained the services of one of Philly's best lawyers, James Coben, to represent La Puta. But the Feds were going all out. They were seeking the death penalty. James Coben advised La Puta to take a deal for life in prison without the possibility of parole.

Once the indictment was unsealed in court, there was no way that La Puta was going to win. When it was the United States of America versus You, it means that they would lie, put people you didn't even know on the stand, produce evidence no one knew existed, and use all their resources to convict you.

Me personally, I was willing to use all my money to fight the government, but since my brother, Li'l Flash, was the government's witness, La Puta decided to cop the fuck out.

Vicky "La Puta" Lopez became the first female in the City of Philadelphia to be given a life sentence under the RICO Act. Seeing my mother in a wheelchair in the courtroom really sent my ass on tilt. I had nothing left in my life to look up to.

My brother, Li'l Flash, was sent to Heavenford Prison, in Montgomery County, Pennsylvania, to do his two years.

A month later . . .

Fatima begged me not to, but I had to do it. I couldn't sleep, eat, or shit. The only thing I kept seeing in my mind was my brother's smiling face. I was about to show him why I was America's worst nightmare. If he thought the walls of prison were gonna keep his snitching ass safe from my reach, he was wrong!

Maggy DeSanchez was a businesswoman in North Philly who had always prided herself on being a top spokesperson for the Hispanic community. To me, she was nothing but a fucking hustler who played on the struggles of poor people. She was also the person who had praised the FBI publicly for taking La Puta off the streets. I could have killed her if I wanted to, but I was only trying to send a message to all the snitches.

One day I waited by her car, which was parked in front of Centro Musical Store. It was broad daylight, and the streets were packed with people.

As Maggy DeSanchez walked toward her car, she smiled, although it was obvious that she sensed that something was wrong. She remained calm, trying to hide the fear traveling through her body. *It's broad daylight! I'm not worried about a thing. That young man is probably an ex-offender looking for a job*, she thought to herself as she reached her car.

"Are you Maggy DeSanchez?" I asked her in a demanding voice while pushing up against her.

"Yes. Why?"

"I was wondering if you could help me."

"I need to know the problem first."

"I just want you to remember that loose lips sink ships!" With one continuous motion, I pulled out a box cutter and slashed her face open. She screamed, but no one dared to get next to me.

When I was done, I sat on the hood of her car, as if nothing had happened. When the police arrived, I just threw my hands up in the air and surrendered.

Maggy DeSanchez was taken to Temple Hospital, where she received 103 stitches to close the wound on her face, and I was taken down to the Roundhouse, the Philadelphia Police Department headquarters at Eighth and Race Street, and charged with assault with a deadly weapon.

Part Two

Chapter Twelve

A Different Kind of War

Rashad

My bus ride to the county jail felt good. As the bus full of prisoners moved down the highway, the iron chains wrapped around my waist and the shackles on my ankles embedded in me a desire for payback. The sound of my mother's voice kept ringing in my ears. *Nigga, you're crazy!*

I looked out the window as miles of freedom passed me by.

Two resentful guards with shotguns sat behind a cage on the bus and eyeballed me, hoping I would attempt to escape. Their eyes were burning through my soul. My hatred toward them was equal to theirs.

Crackas! I'm not one of these clowns on this bus! I want to be here! Society has produced a monster, and now they were gonna have to deal with it! I thought.

When the bus arrived at my new home, I managed to maintain my cool. I was now playing with major players. I felt the eyes of the other walking dead men as I got off the bus.

"Look at the young, pretty one!" I heard one prisoner tell another while pointing in my direction.

I just smiled to myself as I looked straight at the prisoner who had made the statement, letting him know that I was no pussy, faggot, or chump. At that moment, I knew I would have to reach deep into my killa bag and become more vicious than the rest of the niggas at this house of correction. The only thing that mattered to me was that I was one step closer to catching up with my brother.

Once I got assigned to a cellblock, I ran into a nigga from New York, and he blessed me with a banger, a knife. I went to handle my business with the booty bandit who was pointing at me when I was getting off the bus. I embraced my knife with great passion.

The new arrivals were being dogged by the other inmates. Some were assigned to sleep in the day room on the floor until a cell became available. Others were assigned to bunk up with the booty bandits. Most of the clerks were booty bandits, so when new arrivals came in, they selected who they wanted to run up in, and arranged the paperwork so their homies got first selection of the fresh meat in the jail.

Me, I was assigned to bunk up with an old nigga named Bebop, from West Philly. He was the same nigga who had made the faggot remark when I was getting off the bus. The second I stepped into the cell, he got fly with the mouth.

"Young buck, hold the fuck up! The only people allowed in my cell is my bitches!" he said as he got up from his bed and slipped his county boots on.

I just looked at him and placed my box on top of his bunk, just to show him disrespect. I gripped my knife, and without saying a word, I began to stab him the fuck up. I blanked out. I hit the nigga in the neck, arms, and back. When the guards came running, none of them had the heart to grab me.

The entire assault lasted three minutes. When it was over, the booty bandit was unconscious and bleeding like a water fountain.

I was given thirty days in the hole. After that, I had my own cell and control of the cellblock, and I was given the job of phone monitor, assigning phone time to the rest of the inmates.

This house of correction was sort of luxurious. Everything was brought to the cellblocks. COs would sell themselves short in exchange for money.

Not long after my arrival, I had got to know this house of correction like the back of my hand. Just like the streets, I was making a name for myself.

COs and prisoners alike knew I was unpredictable. One day I was cool, and the next day I'd be up in some nigga's cell, beating him upside the head with a shank. It was all about respect.

The niggas in this house of correction were from different parts of the city, and most of them thought they ran the jail, so a geographical turf war was in full effect. Muthafuckas who weren't shit on the streets were now trying to build up their reputations by trying to call the shots and direct what went down on the cellblock. Sometimes prison made people feel needed and important. These were niggas who under normal circumstances didn't amount to shit. But they came to prison and became leaders, jailhouse lawyers, politicians, Muslims, Christians. You name it, and you'd probably find it in here. Prison worked magic for some niggas, and most inmates in here tended to follow the nigga that talked a good game.

The Puerto Ricans in this house of correction were always treated like suckas. The black brothers felt that they wouldn't fight back, because they were few in number. I was not having any of that shit.

Early one morning, this Muslim nigga unsuccessfully tried to take my breakfast tray.

"You, pretty nigga, let me get that tray!"

"Nigga, the only thing you can get is a piece of metal up in you!" I responded.

"I'm tired of you running around here like you run shit! Nigga, this is Philly! You got to pay taxes!" he growled.

"I don't give a fuck how you feel!" I spit my razor out of my mouth and let it slide down his grill.

A mini race riot broke out. Niggas were getting stabbed up and sliced open with razor blades. At the end of the fight, ten inmates and four guards were stabbed up. The Muslims wanted to retaliate, but the Puerto Rican niggas wouldn't back down. I was on my bullshit for real!

Prison administrators separated the Puerto Ricans and the blacks. After that incident, I built a jailhouse gang called CBS, or Can't be Stopped. Every Puerto Rican nigga that came through the jail either got down or was put on the same housing unit with the blacks, which meant they would probably end up fucking or getting their shit taken.

The CBS gang made the guards earn their tax dollars. We made their workplace unsafe for them, like it was supposed to be. These toy cops weren't supposed to come in here and treat grown men like children and feel safe about it. Every time one of the COs went beyond their work duty to fuck with us, they got their head split open as a reminder of where they were at. The same went for those inmate niggas who loved to be up in the police's faces. If they got caught fraternizing, they got their shit split, because sooner or later, they would become informants for the jail.

A month later . . .

I vividly remembered the day a redneck guard came to my cell and abruptly interrupted my peaceful sleep. The banging on the cell door sounded so far away that for a brief second, I thought I was dreaming. But the glaring light beaming in my eyes from a powerful flashlight told me that I wasn't. Then the word *court* escaped his mouth in slow motion.

I was happy as hell, because I knew this would be the day I would plead guilty and be sent to Heavenford Prison, where I would have a well-deserved family reunion with my brother.

Chapter Thirteen

In God We Trust

Rashad

Sitting in the courthouse a half hour before I was to stand trial, I felt like a king. If the courtroom wasn't packed with people, I would have pulled my dick out and beat it. My plan was unfolding just the way I wanted.

The district attorney's office in Philadelphia was interested in only one thing—a conviction. They thought they were going to violate my rights and treat me like most of the criminals. I was hip to their game. I could have retained a twenty-five-thousand-dollar lawyer if I wanted, but it would have defeated my purpose.

I looked around the courtroom and spotted Fatima, Miguelito, Dirty D, Tungo, Crazy Horse, and some other bitches from the Bronx that I had never seen before.

As the judge approached the bench, I felt calm. I had been methodical and was thoroughly prepared for what would happen next.

"Your Honor, the people are ready to begin," the DA said with a smile.

"Does the defendant have counsel?" the judge asked in a nasty voice.

I slowly got up from my chair and asked the judge for permission to speak. "Your Honor, I would like to address the court," I said with a sad look on my face.

"Young man, do you have counsel?"

"No. I don't need any. Your Honor, I would like to enter a plea of guilty. I take full responsibility for hurting Ms. DeSanchez. I want to save the court time and money, so I plead guilty."

"Young man, do you know what you're doing?"

"Your Honor, I have the right to accept responsibility for my actions!"

"Yes, you do. Therefore, the court accepts your guilty plea," the judge replied.

I looked over at Fatima and my team and smiled.

The next day, I was brought back to court, surrounded by ten sheriffs, to receive my sentence.

The judge looked over at me sternly. "Mr. Lopez, taking your guilty plea into consideration, and after hearing from the victim, I impose a sentence of one to three years in state prison. Do you understand me?"

"Yes, I do," I answered.

The judge slammed his gavel down on his bench.

Two days later, I was transported to Heavenford Prison. I was one step closer to avenging my mother.

Chapter Fourteen

Only the Strong Survive

Rashad

Being transferred to Heavenford was like a blessing. I had heard many stories about the place, but I wasn't worried. My mission was to bump heads with my brother. I was determined to endure whatever came my way.

As the bus approached its destination, I could see the forty-foot wall that surrounded the prison. I tried to look around at the landscape surrounding the wall, and for a minute I found myself appreciating the flowers and grass, not because I loved nature, but because I knew it would probably be a while before I saw such landscaping again. Although I had got only one to three years, nothing in prison was for sure, and given what I was planning, I could be looking at a much longer sentence.

The cracks on the walls around the prison made it resemble a concentration camp. I was now entering a world within a world. It was a world where no one could promise a tomorrow.

Out of seven of us on the blue bus, two of the guys were veterans at doing time, so to them, this was a joy ride. Heavenford was the fifth largest state prison in the United States of America, and one of the most dangerous in Pennsylvania, and not too many twenty-year-olds made it out alive. And if they did, they were probably worse off than when they entered.

I was going to do my funky one to three years my way. I had to work quickly, because three years in prison went by fast.

When the bus finally reached its destination, the wall around the perimeter looked much larger up close. Now I could see a guard spitting tobacco juice down on the ground from a gun tower. He held a shotgun in his hand.

Minutes later, the steel gates in the wall cracked open with a wrenching sound, confirming my arrival. As the steel gates closed behind the blue bus, I decided to leave whatever humanity I possessed on the other side of the forty-foot wall.

The other four young niggas on the bus looked at one another, while the two veterans just stared ahead nonchalantly. I was smiling because these four young muthafuckas were afraid. Five of us were coming in, but the question was, "Who was gonna make it out?" If I was a betting man, I'd put money on myself. None of these niggas had the heart I had.

Once we reached intake, also known as the receiving room, we were told to put all our personal property on top of a counter. Next, we were taken to a small shower room, where a white guard stood in a corner, watching and spitting out orders in all directions.

"Rub that shampoo under your balls! We don't want y'all niggers or spics to bring any diseases up in here!" the asshole guard yelled, turning red in the face.

Once we were done, we were given a pair of punk panties (underwear), a pair of brown boots, and a blue jumpsuit. Ten pictures were the only things we were allowed to take to our new domain. I decided to send all my pictures to Fatima. I wanted nothing that reminded me of the streets.

Next, our fingerprints were taken, and we were assigned new identification numbers. In prison, your birth name or nickname didn't mean shit. A number was your new identity, and you'd better remember it!

"Line the fuck up!" a guard yelled at us. Then he added, "If any of y'all have any enemies in the system, speak up now! Once we start moving, I don't want to hear shit! Now, where do y'all want y'all's body sent to, in the event that someone decides to claim it?"

No one spoke up, but I could hear the heartbeats of the other four young niggas. I chuckled softly.

"Damn, nigga! You act like this is funny!" a so-called young killa named Baby Love said to me.

"I'm not scared of anyone, nigga. All these old niggas in here could suck my dick! It is what it is!"

"Boy, did I ask you to speak?" the white guard yelled in my face.

"Fuck you! I do what I wanna do!"

"Oh, we got a tough one here! Let's see how tough you are when you get to the blocks!" he said as we followed him down a long corridor.

The corridor was like four city blocks put together. It had dim lighting, and the smell of death floated in the air.

The older niggas stared at the fresh meat that had just arrived at the "market." By the looks on their faces, they were already making plans for us. I kept my head up and mean mugged every nigga that looked my way.

When we entered Cellblock E, I could swear that I was on a slave plantation. All I saw was cells on top of cells full of Hispanics and blacks. The only white faces belonged to the guards. There were two men to a cell no bigger than eight by twelve feet, and eight hundred niggas to a cellblock. Niggas were packed in like sardines in a can.

COs constantly wanted a nigga to strip for a cavity search to see if he had any hidden contraband in his ass. Showing your dick, balls, and asshole to these clowns in here was a daily routine. It was part of the dehumanizing process. Some of the guards suffered from "little dick syndrome," and it inflamed them when they strip-searched a nigga that had a bigger dick than theirs. I found this out my second day in Heavenford, when a cell search was conducted.

This homo-ass CO nigga walked into my cell and tried to run game down on me. "Mr. Lopez, I'm Officer Jefferson, and I run this block. I checked your books, and you seem to have a lot of money. In here, a few dollars will get your cell door open and extra food."

"Do I look hungry?" I smiled and waited for him to finish running his mouth.

"Oh, you're a tough one, right? Sir, I'm giving you a direct order to strip!"

"I don't give a fuck about stripping," I responded as I took off my jumpsuit.

"Sir, bend over and spread your ass cheeks open. Lift your dick up. Now lift your balls up. Sir, pull the skin of your dick back. Wiggle your toes. Open your mouth . . ."

The entire process was to humiliate you on all levels. That shit y'all saw in the movies or on TV was pure fiction. What I was experiencing in the flesh was real, and there was no director telling me what to do. Even though I didn't like the script, there was nothing I could do to change it. It was either go with the flow or become a victim of the system. The jungle code said that the strong must feed on any prey at hand.

I'd always been a desensitized person. I never let bullshit I couldn't control bother me. This homo-ass nigga had thought that I was gonna refuse to strip. And I had just laughed in his face.

Afterward, my belly was bloated from the plague of hate and homicidal thoughts. Sooner or later, I would get even!

Three weeks later . . .

While awaiting a transfer to Klan Hill, the place where I was supposed to be classified, one of the young niggas who had arrived with me was brutally raped. Baby Love had made the mistake that no new young nigga in prison should ever make. He had befriended a booty bandit and had started accepting cigarettes and commissary from him, not knowing that he was being set the fuck up. He had thought that because they were cellmates, he was cool. The old booty bandit had arranged with the block clerk to have Baby Love raped.

Big Tee knew that in order for him to conquer Baby Love's asshole, he had to gain his trust and make him feel like they were old friends. Since Big Tee wasn't an aggressive booty bandit, he enlisted the help of his partner, Pennsylvania's worst booty bandit. He was six feet four, 330 pounds, and had a solid body, a bald head, white teeth, and a hoarse voice that spoke death every time he opened his mouth. He was known throughout the penal system and among the prisoners as Chocolate Boy. He had an obsession with the smell of shit, and it drove him crazy and mad with desire.

Chocolate Boy was, by all means, made into a monster by the system. At the beginning of his sentence in the county jail, he was raped by three white prison guards. In return, he murdered one of them. He turned a six-month county bid for a nickel bag of marijuana into a life sentence without parole. A year into his life sentence, he raped a male nurse and beat him with a nightstick, leaving him brain dead. For that, he received another life sentence and fifteen years in solitary confinement.

Everyone saw it coming, and I even tried to warn Baby Love about what could happen to him, but the nigga wouldn't listen. His response was always, "Nigga, you're crazy!"

One afternoon, when they opened the cell doors for showers, Baby Love's cellmate, Big Tee, left first. Minutes later, Chocolate Boy ran in his cell with a shank and knocked Baby Love the fuck out, greased him up, and viciously raped him while holding the shank under his neck. When he was done fucking him, he knocked Baby Love out again and walked out of the cell and off the block, as if nothing had happened.

When Baby Love came out of the cell, crying and bleeding, with shit running down his legs, the guards on the bridge immediately knew what had happened and who the perpetrator was. But if they turned Chocolate Boy in, they knew their jobs would be on the line, and they weren't willing to give up their jobs because Baby Love had got raped.

"Shit! Elaski, I told you not to let that nigger up here!" I heard one of the guards tell the main guard in charge.

"Don't worry about it. He's just another spic. Just act like you don't know anything," Officer Elaski responded.

When they asked Baby Love what was wrong, he tried to explain to them that he had been raped, but they were acting as if they didn't believe him.

When a lieutenant was called in, he took his time questioning Baby Love and laughed. "Boy, do you know who raped you?"

"No, sir," Baby Love responded.

The lieutenant asked a few more questions, but since no one had seen or heard anything, there was little he could do. Besides, for the lieutenant, these kinds of incidents were routine. And nine times out of ten, they never caught the perpetrator.

Baby Love was taken to the prison infirmary, where he got his asshole stitched back together. Then he was sent back to his cell.

His cellmate, Big Tee, was acting all concerned but offered no help. The foundation had been laid already. Big Tee had wanted to fuck Baby Love from day one.

I tried to hype Baby Love up so he would stab his cellmate, but he was scared. So afterward, Baby Love became the hottest piece of punk ass in Heavenford. Even the guards were giving him money for sexual favors.

In prison, there was nothing for free. If a muthafucka gave you some commissary, trust me, that commissary came with strings attached to it. Sooner or later, you would have to pay it back in some way. Society's morals and standards didn't mean shit in here. Prison had its own code of ethics, which every inmate had to live by.

The day after Baby Love was raped, I was transferred to Klan Hill to get classified.

Chapter Fifteen

Klan Hill

Rashad

Klan Hill looked more like a college campus from the outside than a correctional institution. In fact, in the early sixties it was called White Hill, which had a collegiate ring to it. To this day, a sign with the original name hung on the front gate, and you saw it when you first entered the damn place.

Unlike at Heavenford, guards had full control at Klan Hill, and a nigga was locked in his cell for most of the day. The only time we were let out was for showers, trips to the dining hall and the yard, guest visits, and time at the commissary. The cellblocks were much smaller than the ones at Heavenford, and they contained two hundred people at the most. There were two niggas to a cell, and no TVs or radios were allowed. The guards on the block basically knew everyone by name and number.

The place was designed to break a nigga down, but since I wasn't the kind of nigga who gave a fuck about authority figures, I made sure the guards knew I didn't care about them.

The soft-ass young niggas who were housed on the same block didn't appeal to me. They were too fucking scared of the guards and of taking a trip to the hole for sixty to ninety days. Their willpower was stripped from them at the front gate.

I knew from day one that Klan Hill was not the place for me.

Racism was rampant. It seemed like the only people of color were the inmates. There were only two or three black or Hispanic guards, and believe me, those assholes were straight up Uncle Tom house niggers. Black and Hispanic guards always went beyond the call of duty. They were trying to impress the white guards by abusing their power, and they didn't realize the white guards they were trying to impress looked at them with disdain. It didn't matter if they wore the same uniform; the white guards would never consider them equals. How could they when they saw how they treated their own kind? In prisons like Klan Hill, black and Hispanic guards were intimidated and feared losing their jobs. For them, working in a prison, inspecting dicks, balls, and assholes, was something major!

Three weeks later . . .

After three weeks in quarantine, the first of many problems crept up on me.

While I was standing in line for the commissary, a nigga from South Philly named Duke was behind me and rubbed his dick against my leg. I ignored him, because the guards were looking in my direction.

That night in my cell, I took two razor blades and melted them onto a toothbrush. That faggot thought he was being clever by telling other niggas that I was gonna be his punk.

The next morning, when they opened the cell doors for breakfast, I grabbed my toothbrush and walked down to his cell. The morning traffic of hungry niggas trying to be first in the dining hall made it easier for me to approach the faggot and go unnoticed by the guards.

His eyes lit up with lust when he saw me standing in front of his cell. "Hey, sweet boy! You decided to stop by and talk to me, huh?" he whispered from his cell as he tied up his brown state boots. He sat on his bed and licked his lips.

I stared at him coldly. A response wasn't necessary. My mind was already made up. I stepped into his cell with my razors in hand and closed the door behind me. His lust-filled eyes never saw the razors coming down across his face. Blood splashed all over my prison blues and onto the floor.

"You fucking spic! I'ma teach your tender ass a lesson!" he hollered and grinned with his yellow teeth as he tried to compose himself.

His threats fell on deaf ears, because as he charged toward me, I swung my razors from his left ear down to his belly. The gash that ran from his ear was enough to kill any sexual desire he had for me. Fear was now taking over his body. His once lust-filled eyes were now telling me he had had enough, but I was determined to finish what he had started.

I kept swinging the razors at him. Everywhere I hit, a gash would open up. He knew that he was no longer fighting for a piece of ass; he was now fighting to save *his* ass.

His attempt to grab my hand was his worst mistake, because my razors were already crossing his palms. He slipped on his own blood, and I followed with a kick to his face. I kept stomping on his face on the dark gray concrete floor until his teeth were flying out of his bloody mouth.

A CO was about to rush into the cell, but his instincts told him not to. He made a U-turn and shut the door back up to prevent anyone from entering. I knew I had a few more minutes before he returned with the goon squad. I kicked dude in the mouth a few more times. I wanted him to remember my face every time he glanced in the mirror.

Thinking like a hard-core convict, I flushed the toothbrush with the razors attached to it down the toilet, leaving no evidence but an unconscious punk bleeding from what seemed like a thousand gashes.

When the goon squad arrived, they couldn't believe what they were seeing. They rushed me, pushed me down on the floor, and cuffed me. After searching the entire cellblock, they couldn't find a weapon. I received ninety days in the hole and a new street charge. But after the first hearing in court, the street charge was thrown out because of the lack of evidence pointing to me as the perpe-trator. The guard's testimony served me well. He said he didn't see anything. There was no evidence fingering me; therefore there was no case against me. If the guard had admitted that he witnessed me cutting the punk up, he would have admitted that he neglected his duty by not making his rounds every fifteen minutes.

In prison, when a person stabbed or cut up a booty bandit, most of the time the prison officials tried to keep the incident within the prison. Booty bandits had documented history, which made it hard for prison officials to prosecute. Stabbing or cutting up a booty bandit was sweet because it was a win-win case.

Pennsylvania wasn't used to a nigga like me. Giving niggas a buck fifty was something unheard of in the Pennsylvania prison system . . . that is, until they decided to put me among a bunch of fake-ass killas. Every altercation I faced was nothing but a stepping-stone toward my ultimate goal.

After I was released from the hole, I was classified to serve the remainder of my time down in Heavenford, but I was put out in general population. I had already been informed by the prison staff that the DOC was gonna make me max out my sentence, which meant that I would have to serve my entire three years.

Normally, a nigga would be mad about this. Me, I was happy, because my job in the Pennsylvania prisons wasn't done yet.

Once on J Block, I was hearing rumors that Duke's friends wanted to retaliate, and I decided to face whatever came my way. Taking PC, protective custody, was out of the question. Therefore, I was willing to kill the next person who invaded my space. I was labeled "incorrigible."

My presence on J Block gave Duke's friends time to rethink their intentions. There were too many young niggas willing to give up some ass without a fight for them to be fucking with me. Once they saw I wasn't the one to be fucked with, they were on my dick. That was what chumps did when they couldn't beat you.

On J Block, I met a few niggas from New York who were serving time for drug dealing out of Philly. One nigga in particular, whose name was Mustafa and who was from the Bronx, looked real familiar. When he introduced himself to me, I stared at him.

"Yo, B. Where do we know each other from?" I asked. *Damn! I know him from somewhere!*

"You don't remember me, shorty? 'Yo, son! Where're you from? What size you wear?' Remember me now?" he said with a smile.

What a small world! I had never thought I would ever bump heads with da nigga I'd stomped when I first got locked up in juvenile! But here I was, face-to-face with Spofford's main bully.

"Blaze! Yeah, I remember you! It's been a long time," I said, wiping my eyes with the sleeve of my shirt.

"Yo, son, we don't have no beef. That shit we went through is in the past. Right now, out here, we're all we got. I've been out here for four years."

"So, you're a Muslim now?"

"I've always been a Muslim. What're you doing out here? Last I heard, you had the South Bronx on smash."

"Long story, but it is what it is. I'm waiting to be transferred down to Heavenford. What about you?"

"I just got kicked out of Greene County for stabbing some cat. These crackas are sending me up to Huntingdon. But believe me, I won't be there long."

Mustafa and I became tight. At first, I had my suspicions of him, but after a while, he became like my family. The nigga was broke and out on his luck. He was what they called a "state baby." He'd been in the system all his life. He was irrelevant to his family and so-called friends. The prison system was designed to kill a nigga like him mentally.

Mustafa and I formed a wolf pack. We did everything together. Haters couldn't stand us, but they were too fucking scared to invade our space. We even celled up together. I trusted him like a brother, because no matter what went down, he had my back.

Since niggas in prison never talked about their time, I never bothered to ask Mustafa how much time he was doing or what he was down for. But I did notice that he never received any mail or visits and that he had no money for commissary.

"Mustafa, I'm about to put my lady on the visiting list. She's gonna be driving up here from New York. I don't want her to drive by herself, so what you think if I have one of her girlfriends pull you out?"

I saw his lips tighten, and he began biting his nails. "Man, I never been on a visit. I don't have no one out there. My mom passed away years ago, son. Whatever you need me to do, I'll do."

"Nigga, I just want you to enjoy yourself."

"That's mad love, son!" Mustafa said.

"Tell me something. What's poppin' with your case? How much time you got left?" I asked him.

"I'm done, nigga. These people gave me life. I got four in on that. With no lawyer, you know these white people ain't trying to hear nothing a nigga's got to say."

"Yo, B. I know niggas in here make all kinds of promises to niggas, but my word is bond. I got a few extra dollars dat I could throw your way for a lawyer to help you get your time cut. I need you out there on my team. When my lady comes up, I'ma have her contact a friend of mine who's a hot lawyer in Philly."

"Yo, son, I copped a deal. I pled guilty."

"B, money talks and bullshit walks. I'm sure the lawyer will find something to get you back in court."

"But I won't be able to pay you back."

"Nigga, now you're insulting me! You're treating me like a crab nigga!"

"Nah, son. I'm just being real with you."

"Listen here. I know what it feels like to be on both sides of the fence. Whatever I do for you is because I want to do it."

Mustafa was seized with a sudden desire to cry.

"Yo, B! Don't go soft on me!" I said.

Once I got Fatima on my visiting and phone list, I gave her a call and arranged a visit for the following week. I instructed her to have her girlfriend Brenda pull Mustafa out for a visit.

Brenda was a freak bitch who hung around with Fatima. She got ass for days and wouldn't mind getting down. Her brain game was crazy. She knew that I was Fatima's man, but she didn't mind letting me hit it on the down low. She was my stress relief. Whenever I wanted to have a threesome or a straight fuck, she was always available. So, when I wrote her a letter, asking her to pull Mustafa out for a visit, she was game.

April 24, 2004, visiting day . . .

Mustafa and I were up early, waiting for our visits. I wanted to see Fatima real bad. It had been a while since I had last seen her—actually, seven months—because of all the time I'd been in the hole. I didn't want her traveling alone through these racist counties in the middle of nowhere, so I was glad Brenda was accompanying her.

Fatima arrived early. At 9:00 a.m. the guard came to our cell and keyed us out. "Both of y'all assholes got visits! Speed it up!"

Officer Webster was a fucking Uncle Tom nigga who stayed trying to make a nigga's bid hard. He went out of his way to create problems.

"Man, I swear, one of these days that nigga's gonna make me jump on his ass!" Mustafa said as he grabbed his ID card and put a dab of Muslim oil behind his ears.

"Damn, nigga! You act like you're going out on a date!" I said with a smile. I could tell that he was nervous. Throughout his entire bid, he'd never been on a visit.

"You never know who might feel the kid out there!" he responded.

Out in the visiting strip, I immediately spotted Fatima and Brenda standing by the vending machine. Damn! Fatima was looking sexy as hell! Brenda and Fatima were both wearing black Gucci dresses. Fatima ran up to me and hugged me when she saw me heading in her direction. Her body pressed against me gave me an instant hard-on. *I got to get a shot of pussy!*

"Hey, baby! You look good!" I said to her, feeling her nipples pressing against my chest.

"You don't look too bad. You gained a li'l bit of weight. I can't wait until you come home!" Fatima said. Her eyes were getting watery.

"By the way, dis is my main man, Mustafa, otherwise known as Blaze. He's from down da way. Mustafa, dis is Brenda and Fatima. Now, y'all two go find a seat while I holla at Fatima for a minute," I said. I gave Brenda a hug and let her feel my hard-on while Fatima was grabbing a food tray.

"Damn, nigga! I wish I could suck your dick right here! You know, Fatima and I ain't wearing any panties! Maybe you could feel my pussy!" Brenda whispered in my ear.

"Nah, baby. Once I bounce from here, I'll hit dat. But listen. Make my homeboy feel good. He's been down for a while. Give him a wet finger."

"I got you, *papi*!" Brenda said as Fatima walked over with a tray of vending machine food. She had chicken wings, pizza, soda, and a Snickers candy bar.

"What are you two talking about?" she asked Brenda as she led me to the seats she wanted to sit on.

"Nothing. I was just asking Rashad a few questions about his friend."

"Girl, stop acting shy. Go entertain that nigga for a while. I seen him looking at your ass!" Fatima said with a smile.

"I think he's scared of me," Brenda responded.

"Nah. My man is just a respectable man. Once you talk to him, he'll open up," I said, trying to get Brenda away from us.

Brenda

"Mustafa, why don't we get something to snack on? Then you could tell me a little bit about yourself," I said as I walked in front of him, shaking my ass hard. I didn't even have to look back to know he was hawking my fat ass. I caught a few niggas looking over their women's shoulders just to get a peek at me. When I was in front of the vending machines, I turned around and asked him, "What do you want to eat?"

"Anything but pork."

"Oh, you one of those Muslims?"

"Nah. Pork just makes me sick."

"You eat fish?" I asked in a provocative way.

"Only if it's clean!"

Okay, the nigga ain't as slow as he looks. I'ma see how he's gonna react when I show him my shaved pussy. I bet he cums on himself! I thought as I bent down to pick up my ID card, which I had dropped on purpose.

Once I had got all the food we were gonna eat, we sat down. I placed the food tray on my lap so Mustafa would have to reach over to grab whatever he wanted. While he ate his fish sandwich, I snacked on a bag of popcorn. Little by little, I pulled the front of my dress up, exposing my shaved pussy.

I placed a Coke bottle between my legs. The cold bottle sent chills over my pussy. When Mustafa reached over to grab the soda, I held his hand. "If you grab the soda now, you might be exposed to something special!" I said, letting his hand go.

When he grabbed the soda and looked between my legs, my pussy was winking at him. "Damn!" was the only thing he said.

"How long has it been since you seen any pussy?" I asked him.

"A long time!"

"So, what? You just gonna look at it?" I asked, wanting to get freaky right in the visiting room. The thought of exposing myself to a nigga that was restricted from everything a normal muthafucka took for granted had me feeling horny.

Mustafa placed his hand over my lap, then let his fingers slide into my pussy, two fingers, then three, then four . . . while he used his thumb to rub my clit.

Rashad

"Do you know when you're getting transferred? Baby, I want you home real bad. I miss you."

"I should be outta here in a few weeks. Trust me, it will be over soon. Have you heard from my mom?" I asked while peeping the freak shit my nigga Mustafa was doing. *Damn! The nigga already has his hands full!*

"I went to visit her last week. I flew down to the Federal Bureau of Prisons' medical facility in Fort Worth, Texas, where they got her housed. She's doing good. Still in the wheelchair. I put five grand in her commissary books, because in a few weeks she should be getting her prosthetic leg, and she's got to pay for it if she wants it."

"Did she ask about me?"

"Yeah, she did. She don't know you're locked up. As far as she's concerned, the Feds don't let you visit her. You know them assholes do background checks on people visiting their institutions. She told me that she requested special permission to have you placed on her visiting list."

"How's she gonna manage that?"

"She's got a male friend, a guard, who's gonna bypass all the red tape. Don't ask me who he is, 'cause she didn't say."

"Anyway, what's up with you?"

"I'm holding it down. Miguelito's still got the block on lock. Grip and Dirty D come by the house every day. Money is stacking up like crazy."

"Look, baby. Before I forget, take thirty grand and go see that lawyer in Philly, James Coben. Tell him that if he takes my nigga Mustafa's case, gets it back in court, and gets his time cut to no more than six years, I'll give him another thirty."

"Damn, baby! You ain't even paid that much for you! Who the fuck is that nigga?"

"Dat nigga ain't got nobody out there. He's da nigga dat I trust with my life in here. He's like a brother to me. He would do da same for me if he had it."

"You don't have to get so emotional! I'll take care of that as soon as I leave here. Consider it done." Fatima turned her head and saw Brenda jerking Mustafa off. "What the fuck!" she said.

"Mind your business, baby!" I told her with a smile and pinched her nipples.

"Don't do that! It makes my pussy wet!" Fatima said as I slid my hand under her dress and started playing with the pussy.

"Let's fuck, baby," I said to her while she laid her hand on my dick.

"If we get busted, you'll lose your visits."

"Who cares? I'm out dis place in a few weeks anyway." With that said, I pulled my dick out of my jumpsuit and pulled her dress up as she sat on my lap. She positioned her pussy so that she could press down on my dick. At first, it only touched her pussy lips. Then it pressed against them. The head of my dick made contact with her clit. The roundness of my dick pushed against her little clit and set it quivering.

"Baby, I haven't had any dick since you left me," she whispered in my ear as I pushed up, trying to drive my dick deeper into her.

I looked over at Brenda, and she smiled when she saw Fatima sitting on my lap. Suddenly, Brenda got up and bent over the chair, and Mustafa stood behind her and gave her what she wanted—some jailhouse dick!

Fatima's pussy contracted around my dick and coated it with her juice. I shot my way overdue cum deep into her for what seemed like hours.

Suddenly, I saw two guards running into the visiting room. At first, I thought they were coming for me and Mustafa, but when one of the guards didn't try to stop Mustafa, I instantly knew that something major was popping off. Normally, the guards in the visiting room were like hawks, standing over niggas and watching everything.

Around 2:00 p.m., we saw a guard running past the visiting-room yard, holding his head together. Five minutes later, ten guards rushed into the visiting room with guns in their hands and escorted all the visitors out of the institution.

The guard in the visiting room wouldn't tell us what was happening, but we knew that a riot was jumping off. I was sad because I was missing the opportunity to fuck up a few guards.

We were kept locked in the visiting room for five hours that day. Only after niggas began breaking into the vending machines did they lead us out of the visiting room through a side door to C-Block yard, where we were cuffed up and thrown on the fucking ground.

Finally, at midnight, they decided to take us back to the cellblocks. Once there, Mustafa and I got the entire story from other prisoners on what had sparked the uprising.

Chapter Sixteen

Riot Time

Mustafa

The next morning the staff at Klan Hill made the mistake of opening the cell doors for breakfast. To them the riot the day before was nothing but an isolated incident.

Nigga poured out of their cells for breakfast, as if they'd been starving for years. Everyone had that "something's gonna happen" look on their faces. What was unusual about this particular morning was that the entire inmate population was eating breakfast.

The older niggas were all crowded up at the front of the chow hall, and the young niggas were ready for war but were looking for some guidance from the old heads. The old heads wanted to meet with prison officials to discuss ways to reduce tension in the inmate population.

Me, personally, I didn't give a fuck either way, because once shit got hot, the old niggas were gonna tell. Old heads in prison today disliked the younger breed of prisoners, because in their eyes, we were too radical, so it was nothing to sell one of us out in a heartbeat. In my eyes, they were the biggest snitches in the state. I'd rather fight than have a snitch-ass old head sell me the fuck out.

COs were standing in front of the main gate, harassing a young nigga who was refusing to tuck in his shirt. Words were exchanged, and a rookie CO with less than six months on the job grabbed the young nigga by the neck and yelled, "I'm not going to tell you again to tuck your shirt in now! Nigger, you're not in the hood! This is a direct order!"

A crowd of young niggas started surrounding him.

Sergeant Bubba, a fat, nasty white man who prided himself on being a ball breaker of the Hispanics and blacks, saw the rookie CO being surrounded and decided to play hero. "Gentlemen, break it up, and that's a direct order!" Sergeant Bubba Baker pushed his way through the crowd and stood beside the rookie guard. "Let's move it now! It's time to return to the cellblocks now! Move it, niggers!" he yelled and then spit a ball of chewing tobacco on a young nigga's boots.

"Free fall!" yelled another inmate in the crowd, and all hell broke loose.

The prisoners started whipping the guards' asses. Within five minutes, they had full control of the entire jail and had taken ten hostages. Since prison officials considered Klan Hill a juvenile facility, they thought they could restore order without notifying the state police. Since there was no organization, prison officials managed to get some of the old heads to convince the young niggas to go back to their cells.

By 7:30 p.m., niggas began to get tired and voluntarily returned to their cells. The warden took that as a sign of weakness and refused to meet with the so-called inmate leaders. The guards, on the other hand, thought they had regained control of their domain, and they were showing their asses off. That sense of power gave them heart.

The morning after, April 26, 2004 . . .

This morning the warden's face appeared on the screen of every inmate's TV, and those who didn't have a TV got the chance to hear him over the loudspeakers on every block.

"Good morning, gentlemen! My name is Superintendent Freeman, and I'm the warden of this institution."

"Today I was given a list of demands from the inmate population, and after reviewing them with the internal staff and colleagues, we took the time to compare those demands with our current rules and regulations of this institution. We concluded that there are no flaws in our current policy. Therefore, we will not give in to the demands of the inmate population. Yesterday's disturbance was an isolated incident that has been brought under control. Those inmates involved will be identified and dealt with accordingly, and they will possibly face additional street charges. Gentlemen, we expect you to cooperate with your block officer so that we can get this institution back to its normal functioning."

A collective silence fell over Klan Hill. Everyone knew what had to be done. The situation was do or die.

The COs were planning to retaliate, with deadly force, against the entire inmate population. Their anxiousness to release their anger was so high that they had failed to realize that the levers on the control boxes on every block had been ripped off the walls. They assumed that because the inmates were locked in their cells, the jail was secure. All the inmates had to do was open the cell doors and walk out of their cells.

The COs were planning to creep up on us that night. They were communicating through their radios, and some inmates had possession of radios, so we knew all about their plan ahead of time. We weren't about to sit around and wait. If we did, there was no doubt that some of us would be killed.

7:30 p.m. that same night . . .

The racist guards were forced to pass out doggie-bag dinners to all the inmates. Suddenly, all the lights went out, and every inmate's radio was tuned to the same station. The guards were panicking in the middle of the dark cellblocks.

Big House, a six-foot-four-inch black nigga with a whole lot of anger in him, slid out of his cell with the quickness of a snake and crawled on his stomach to the middle of the cellblock, where two racist guards were trying to hide. The guards never felt Big House's presence. With a nightstick that he had taken from a guard the day before in his hand, he began to beat both of the two fearful guards over their heads. One of them was knocked out with the first blow, and the other one remained on his feet, begging for his life.

"Please don't do this to me! I've got a family! I've never done anything wrong to you guys!"

His words excited Big House to the point where he wanted to rip the guard's head off his shoulders. Big House was having too much fun doing to the guards what they had done to him for the past fifteen years. "You shoulda thought about your family when you wrote me up, bitch!"

Big House's harsh words were all the guard needed to hear to understand that Big House was one angry nigga and was ready to kill him if he kept begging and pleading for his life.

"Bitch-ass cracka! Open your mouth!" Big House ordered. Then he pulled out his big black dick and urinated in the guard's mouth. "Bitch! You better swallow it, 'cause if you don't, I'm gonna kill your white ass!" This shit was personal for him. All the misconducts and street charges the guards at Klan Hill had fabricated against him were now flashing through his mind.

After the guard finished swallowing what seemed like a gallon of raw nigga piss, Big House started striking him over the head with the same nightstick they had used on him on a number of occasions. "Bitch, you're lucky I need this stick! If not, I would shove it up your ass!" he whispered as he cuffed the two guards to the bars of another nigga's cell door.

Click! Click! Click!

The sounds of the cell doors opening were heard in unison. Everything happened so quickly, the guards never had a chance to run. Twenty guards were taken hostage, stripped of their power, and dressed in prison clothes. They were spread throughout the institution, making any attempt to rescue them difficult.

Like the night before, the jail once again went up in flames. Only this time, there was more organization. Missions were handed out to groups of inmates. Niggas were dispatched to patrol the back of the cellblocks to make sure no other guards were hiding. Inmate snitches were also rounded up. Nightsticks, shields, Mace, tear-gas masks, and handcuffs were used to detain the guards.

Of the twenty-five guards that were held hostage, twenty of them were associated with the KKK. The other five were just in the wrong line of work. The KKK guards were violated in the most degrading ways. They were beaten with hammers, nightsticks, bats, iron bars, weight bars, and with whatever else was at hand at the moment. The same humiliation they'd inflicted upon the inmates was now being inflicted upon them.

Officer Webster was one of the most vicious niggers on the face of the planet. He would disrespect inmates' families for no reason, terminate their visits, and he would fabricate misconducts. He was just a miserable nigger that had no right to be in this world. He had never thought that one day all the shit that he had done to the inmates would come back to bite him on the ass. He caught the worst deal of his life. The power the correctional officer's uniform gave him was now shifted to the hands of those he despised so much.

"Lay dat nigga facedown! We going to teach him a lesson!" said Money, a nigga from South Philly, instructing the two skinhead white boys who were holding Webster by the neck.

Once Officer Webster was on the ground and spread eagle, a masked white boy raped the shit out of him and infected him with AIDS. "How do you like that, nigger? Since you want to be white, take this white dick in your black ass, nigger! Maybe next time you'll act like a nigger instead of white!" Jimmy, the masked inmate, was talking mad shit.

It wasn't often that the blacks requested Jimmy's services. The fact that he was given the green light by the blacks to do whatever he wanted to Officer Webster was enough for him to make this opportunity count.

The blacks and Hispanics enjoyed the scene. Once Jimmy was done, he stuffed Officer Webster's shitty and bloody punk panties in his mouth. Then he broke a broomstick in half and shoved the jagged part up Webster's ass, to the max. The other guards watched in disbelief. The inmate snitches were given the same treatment or worse.

Everywhere you looked that day, you would see thirty to forty booty bandits standing in line, waiting to get their dick sucked by some freak-ass homo or guard.

The only thing all the inmates had in common for those three days was that they were all tired of the abuse and ill treatment that occurred on a daily basis at Klan Hill. Some niggas were taking their frustrations out on other inmates with weight-lifting bars and pipes. Those who hid in their cells were beaten, stabbed, and broken the fuck up, because they were considered potential snitches.

Some of the old heads—the so-called leaders in the jail—turned themselves in to the state troopers. They were stripped naked, handcuffed behind their backs, taken to the main yard, and watered down violently with fire truck hoses. Some were beaten nearly to death by the state troopers.

Officer Kim Moore from out of Cook Township, Pennsylvania, the only black female guard at Klan Hill, voluntarily lined up all the young niggas she thought were the organizers of the riot and gave all of them some bomb-ass head. After a while, she dropped her pants down and allowed certain niggas to smash the pussy from all angles. Niggas that hadn't seen pussy in years were now getting their dicks wet, and they were loving it. She ran through fifty niggas before she was allowed to go free, and she never reported her experience. She was a natural-born whore who had fulfilled her fantasy. For the seven years she had been a correctional officer, she'd been fucking with nothing but white boys, but after the young niggas took her pussy, she realized how much she had missed black dick.

After three days of the inmates going hard on the guards, five thousand state troopers armed with guns stormed into the jail and took control. Niggas were either dragged or carried out to the main yard, where they were handcuffed and forced to lie face-first on the wet grass. Payback time was in full effect, and not too many niggas were prepared for the aftermath of the riot.

State troopers formed a line and reviewed the inmates. Inmates who were believed to be the organizers of the riot were taken and dragged around the yard by horses, beaten, then thrown face-first onto a pile of horse shit. Other niggas were randomly selected for this treatment too. This was the strategy the state troopers imposed to plant fear in the inmates.

Some of the guards who had been assaulted were back in the main yard, with their personal guns aimed at the inmates. If one of those crackas didn't like you, most likely, they would select you for the ass whipping of your life and a new street charge, even if you hadn't participated in the riot. Some of the guards wanted to kill us, but the state troopers elected to torture us rather than kill us. The reason for this "leniency" was that a news media helicopter was flying over the yard. If it wasn't, America we would have been blessed with another Attica massacre.

Klan Hill officials had no place to house the three thousand inmates sitting out in the yard, because half of the jail had been burned to the ground. That night, they brought buses into the main yard and loaded them up with inmates and transported us to other correctional institutions around the state.

Those unfortunate inmates who weren't transferred were tortured, given no food, and were forced to sleep in the yard for five nights with nothing but a paper blanket. They were handcuffed behind their backs and were given no opportunity to use the bathroom. All pride was put to the side, and prisoners were actually pulling and holding other niggas' dicks in their hands while they urinated or cleaned their asses. Some kufi-wearing, fake niggas were tucking their kufis under their asses for fear that they'd be identified as Muslims and beaten the fuck down.

Rashad and I were thrown on a bus and transferred out. If we had stayed, we decided that we would have stood our ground and faced the music. There was no way in hell either of us was gonna break down like a bitch and hold a nigga's dick or clean his ass. Fuck that! We're too gangsta for that shit!

Rashad and I ended up getting transferred to Western Penitentiary, out in Pittsburgh, Pennsylvania.

Chapter Seventeen

Solitary Confinement

Rashad

As the bus pulled up to Western Penitentiary, I smiled to myself, because to me, I was one step closer to reuniting with my snitching-ass brother.

Western Penitentiary was the oldest correctional institution in the Commonwealth of Pennsylvania and the second largest facility in the state. But for Mustafa and me, it was like breaking loose from hell.

As the bus approached Pittsburgh, we heard the CO on the bus radio telling the COs at our destination that we were the ringleaders of the riot. That statement alone automatically gave the guards license to do whatever they desired to punish us. We knew we were minutes away from getting our asses beat by the guards.

When the yellow bus entered the institution, I could see the goon squad lined up in riot gear. Physically, I knew I could beat any of those out-of-shape "nigros" they had lined up. But with our hands cuffed behind our backs, there wasn't much we could do.

Once the bus door swung open, a big country nigga from out of Pittsburgh jumped in my face and unleashed a verbal attack on me with his nightstick in hand. "I want one of y'all shit heads to try to take over this jail! This is not Klan Hill, dick heads! Try me! How about you, pretty boy?" he yelled in my face while standing toe to toe with me and spitting all over my face.

"Take these cuffs off and I'll give you a fair one, pussy!" I responded with anger.

"I'll tell you what. I'm going to make your wish come true. Uncuff him now!" he instructed a black female guard who looked like her ass was in her stomach. That was how fat she was.

If this bitch nigga thinks he can beat me, he's in trouble! Since dis nasty chick wants to do a man's job, I'ma knock her out first just for being in the way! I thought to myself as she took her time taking the cuffs off me. The second she was done, I punched the shit out of her jaw and knocked her out cold.

Then I directed my anger at the nigga who wanted to fight. Once I body beat him, he was out of breath. I kept punching his big mouth until he went down on one knee. When he saw that he couldn't do shit with me, he yelled for the other guards to help him. Within seconds, six guards in riot gear were on top of me, beating the living hell out of me. They knew that once daylight came and word got out to general population that an inmate had been beaten up by the goon squad, the prisoners would want to react.

Niggas in other prisons across the state were already feeling humiliated and cheated that the young niggas down at Klan Hill had taken the "crown of glory" from the so-called radical prisoners in the state. The Klan Hill riot wasn't supposed to have happened. Klan Hill was considered by the older inmates in the state prison to be a jail for young niggas with football numbers, for snitches, and for faggots. But while older niggas in other prisons had been playing basketball and fucking punks, us young niggas had been putting in work on these bitch-ass crackas.

The next morning, once word had got out to general population, the Nation of Islam—that is, its security wing, the FOI,—lined up in front of North Block, the hole, solitary confinement, and demanded to see us. Prison officials feared that they might have another riot on their hands. They knew these brothers were ready for action if they didn't let them see us. Two members of the Nation were allowed to come into the hole to see us.

One of them, Brother Ali X 24, addressed us. "Assalamu alaikum. My name is Brother Ali X 24, and I'm the minister of the Nation of Islam. I'm here to ensure y'all's safety." He and his colleague walked around distributing soap, toothpaste, and many other necessary items.

The guards were angry that the administration allowed the FOIs to do this, but they also knew the state couldn't afford another riot so soon.

About the same time that Brother Ali X 24 was walking up and down the hole in Western Penitentiary as if he was Malcolm X, a bus loaded with prisoners was pulling into Heavenford Prison. The twenty-five blacks and five Hispanics on the bus knew what was about to jump off. When the bus arrived at the old restricted housing unit, the RHU, forty-five prison guards in riot gear surrounded the bus and the catwalk leading to the RHU. What the guards didn't know was that officials up at Klan Hill had sneaked an undercover state trooper onto the bus to infiltrate the inmates and see if he could identify the riot participants.

When the bus doors swung open, the prison guards in riot gear stormed onto the bus like the savages they were, beat the prisoners with batons and snapped handcuffs on them.

Julio Cruz, a Hispanic prisoner who was critically ill with AIDS, was dragged out of the bus by his hair, kicked in his balls, and stripped naked. A baton was shoved up his ass as off duty correctional officers stood by cheering the guards who were carrying out this vicious assault on Julio Cruz.

"How does it feel, you dirty spic?" CO Jackson yelled out as he twisted the baton in Julio's ass.

"Don't cry now, *amigo*!" another CO shouted while he pressed his boot against Julio's face.

"Don't hurt 'em too bad, boys!" Sergeant Roche would yell from time to time as he sat in a chair inside the RHU, entertaining himself.

The four angry guards assaulting Julio eventually realized that he wasn't moving, making any attempt to cover the blows that were crushing his already weakened body, or putting up any resistance, unlike the other inmates. Yet they kept on beating him.

"This one is done, boss! I think he passed out. We worked him up pretty good," CO Jackson said to Sergeant Roche, who had come outside by then.

"Fuck him! Secure him in a cell," Roche responded, then ordered four guards to drag Julio by his feet like a pig into a dirty, putrid cell that the sun's light couldn't penetrate.

Handcuffed and shackled at their feet, sixteen of the twenty-five prisoners, including the undercover state trooper, were severely beaten.

"Man, we did a number on those niggers!" Sergeant Roche told the guards after they had all the inmates secured in their cells.

"Roche, some of the guys are going to need some medical attention," Officer Thomas said, wondering if it would ever be traced back to him that he was one of the officers who had assaulted the Hispanic inmates. *Fuck it! I was only following the orders of my superior officer. I wonder if these crackers would've acted the same way had all the guards that got assaulted up in Klan Hill been black? Fuck it! I got to support my white colleagues*, he thought.

"Let the next shift deal with them. As far as I'm concerned, they arrived here from Klan Hill in the condition they're in now. Plus, who's going to believe those dirty bastards?" Sergeant Roche said.

All the guards broke out in laughter while wiping the sweat from their foreheads.

The next morning, when the six-to-two shift arrived, they were unaware of the brutal feast that Sergeant Roche's crew had had the night before. As they made their normal rounds, the reality of the situation unfolded.

When CO Davis reached Julio Cruz's cell, he noticed that the prisoner was on the floor, motionless. When he called a nurse to report what he had discovered, he knew that shit was about to get ugly, and he didn't want any part of it.

"The fucking guards beat the shit out of us! Call my superior officer! I'm a state trooper!" Jason Golden said to one of the guards, who was looking at him as if he was out of his mind.

"Calm down, sir! The nurse will be over to see you in a minute," CO Davis responded, not wanting to believe what he was hearing.

"Sir, I'm not playing or making this up! Here is the phone number of my superior officer. Don't get caught up in something you don't have anything to do with."

Jason Golden was escorted from his cell to the office of the superintendent of the prison. The shit hit the fan when the superintendent called the chief of the state police to inquire why they had sent a state trooper to his facility.

The guards who took part in the savage beating were all denying that a beating had ever taken place. An investigation by the FBI was ordered, and fifteen guards were ultimately charged with murder and with violating the inmates' civil rights.

On July 6, 2005, Sergeant Roche was subpoenaed to testified before a grand jury for the United States district court regarding the death of Julio Cruz and the civil rights violations perpetrated against the inmates during the April 26, 2005, incident at Heavenford. Sergeant Roche lied about his participation in the events of that day.

Two weeks later, he was indicted for murder, and they couldn't stop him from talking. Roche told the court everything he knew about the incident, and shit that wasn't related to the case. "I'm not going down for this alone!" he said to no one in particular as he adjusted the microphone after taking a seat in the witness stand.

Evita Ludwig was a dark-skinned prosecutor with eighteen years' experience. Her body language spoke fear to those who had been unfortunate enough to step in her personal space. Although she was in her late forties, she appeared much younger. Her dark blue eyes and long red hair were evidence that she was racially mixed. Her mother was black, and her father was a racist Red Cross manager who loved himself a piece of dark meat. She met her father for the first time when she was twenty-five. She embraced him and allowed him to be part of her life until he passed away from cancer. It was known around the federal courthouse in Philadelphia that Miss Ludwig was the blackest white woman on the face of the earth.

Hate for the black man was in her blood. She hated men in uniform, cops and prison guards period. She carried her father's hate with a sense of dignity. If a man wasn't a white man, he wasn't right for her.

"Mr. Roche, is it correct that you made false declarations before the grand jury when you stated that you saw nothing unusual on the day Julio Cruz was murdered by your guards?"

"That is correct."

"Is it correct that Julio Cruz was beaten to death because your officers wanted to retaliate for the riot up at Klan Hill?"

"Yes, that's correct."

"Who gave the order for this assault to take place? Who was calling the shots that night?"

"I'm only a sergeant. I follow orders as they come down through the chain of command. I was ordered by Major Lucas to instruct my unit officers to 'have some fun' when the Klan Hill inmates arrived. Major Lucas gave the order."

"And you followed those orders to the T?"

"Yes, I did."

"Who murdered Julio Cruz?"

"As I said in my statement, Major Lucas gave the orders, but Officers Jackson, Thomas, Rivera, and Paulin were the ones who beat Julio Cruz to death. They had the choice of not participating in the beating. It's a known fact around the DOC that inmates get beat down when they arrive in the RHUs for assaulting the guards. Some officers refused to participate, while others wanted to be part of it and have some fun. These four officers requested to have a little fun, as Major Lucas instructed."

"So, the inmates get beat on a regular basis?"

"Yes, they do."

"Is it a policy that inmates must get beaten when they arrive at the RHU?"

"Yes and no. No, because there is no written policy instructing that kind of behavior. And yes, because in the DOC, there are many unwritten policies, policies that prison guards make up to fit a certain situation, and beating up inmates is one of those policies. It strikes fear in the inmates. It lets the inmate population know that if you put your hands on a guard, we will deal with you in a brutal way."

"And who deals with the guards when *they* violate the rules?"

"No one. We run the institution. We devise the rules and policies as we see fit."

"Does this include murder?"

"Yes. It's not the first time that this has happened, and it won't be the last. Even after this unfortunate situation is over, inmates are still going to be beaten and murdered within the walls of the DOC. It's a dirty job."

"Unfortunate for whom?"

"The system, I guess."

"So, are you breaking the code of silence because you care?"

"No. I'm breaking the code of silence because I don't want to be the fall guy for the bigwigs in the DOC. I'm not going down for this by myself."

"But you were the senior officer in your unit, right?"

"Yes, I was."

"So, *you* gave the orders to Officers Thomas, Rivera, Jackson, and Paulin to have some fun?"

"I only did what I was told to do by Major Lucas!"

Sergeant Roche was convicted of second-degree murder, along with seven other guards. While awaiting sentencing at the federal detention center in Downtown Philadelphia, he hanged himself with his bedsheets. Rumors among the prisoners and guards in Heavenford were that he was fucked in the ass by a mob of skinheads at the federal detention center who felt that he had betrayed the KKK for ratting out his coworkers.

Two weeks after my arrival at Western Penitentiary, Mustafa was shipped out to Huntingdon State Prison, and I was transferred to the federal penitentiary in Lewisburg, Pennsylvania.

Chapter Eighteen

Lewisburg Penitentiary

Rashad

Since I was a state prisoner being housed in a federal penitentiary, they dumped my ass in the hole. Solitary confinement became part of my fed time. Every institution I was transferred to, I was placed in the hole because a Klan Hill official had put a letter in my record stating that I was one of the ringleaders in the Klan Hill riot.

Lewisburg Penitentiary was nothing but a star on my "hood jacket," another step to fame among the prisoners, because not too many young niggas wanted to be in prison, let alone in a United States penitentiary. If you survived at Lewisburg, then you could survive in any prison in America.

I am built for dis shit! I wish one of these old niggas would step to me with some punk shit, so

*I could air them the fuck out! If dis is what I gotta
suffer just to get near my brother, so be it. In
the meantime, I must stay on top of my game*, I
thought as I was being escorted to the hole.

Once in my cell, I felt like an animal in a cage.
The cell I was put in was like a boiler room. Pipes
were everywhere, there was no window, and over
my bed was a hot light, which stayed on twenty-four hours a day. Every meal was brought to my
cell. I wasn't allowed to leave for anything except
for showers twice a week.

Immediately, some old Cuban nigga wanted to
get friendly, so I made my position clear to him. I
wasn't trying to hear any bullshit jailhouse game
being spit my way. "Old head, no disrespect, but
I'm not looking for a friend, feel me?"

"Young boy, all y'all little motherfuckers that
come through here always talk that same shit! If
you're not looking for a friend, then maybe you're
looking for a daddy! If not, fuck you!"

"Old head, chill with da loose lips! I haven't
disrespected you. I'm just saying—"

"Nah, little punk! Fuck you, your mama, and
whoever you love! I'm Joey Goya, in case you want
to see me later on."

This old muthafucka was flipping out on me
for no reason. He was either crazy or had a mad
heart. The bitch-ass Cuban boy had me steaming.
Although the consequences for this kind of viola-

tion could mean death, the reality was I probably would never see the nigga again. But just in case, I wanted him to know who I was.

"Old head! I see you are a cell gangsta, talking mad shit! I'm Rashad Lopez from the Bronx, the son of La Puta. And if we ever bump heads, believe me, I'ma cap your old-ass wig back!" I said, lying in bed. The old Cuban boy snapped out, talking shit and calling me all kinds of names.

A lot of the Cuban prisoners who came over to the United States in 1980 were still being held in federal prisons across the country. Most of them wouldn't ever see the streets again, so they didn't care whether they lived or died. Most of them went after the weakest prisoners. Cubans in federal prisons had a vicious reputation for stabbing muthafuckas and taking young boys' asses. But today this old muthafucka had met his match. He was going to be my ticket out of Lewisburg Penitentiary.

"Young boy!" I heard a deep voice say.

At first, I tried to ignore it, but whoever was calling me was persistent.

"Rashad, my name is Santiago Colon. I'm Puerto Rican and also from the Bronx. I heard you going at it with the old Cuban faggot a few doors down. Trust me, he talks shit to everybody that comes through here because he knows he's never going to bump heads with them. But if you really want to go at his neck, I could make it happen tomorrow morning, when they call for showers."

I wondered if he was another booty bandit trying to run some lame-ass game on me, so I responded in a real arrogant manner. "Old head, I'm not looking for any new friends!"

"Young blood, calm down! I'm not your enemy. I saw you when they were bringing you in, and I couldn't help but wonder why they were putting you in here when you look so young. In case you don't know, we are the only two Puerto Ricans up in this piece. So, I hope you don't have a lot of time on your back."

I still doubted him, but I wanted to know what part of the Bronx he was from. "Where in the Bronx are you from, old head?" I asked.

"One-forty-ninth and Prospect Avenue."

"Dat's where I'm from!"

"For real?"

"Yeah!"

"Who are you related to, young blood?"

"I don't have a family. It's just me and my mother, and she's dead," I lied, because I had learned a long time ago never to reveal family names or any kind of information to anyone in prison. Niggas in prison were dirty. You told someone where your family was from, and the next thing you knew, they were getting robbed or killed because a nigga in prison.

"Sorry to hear that."

"What are you in for?"

"I took a case for my old head. A federal gun charge. Five to ten years."

"How about you? Who are you related to?" I asked.

"I got a daughter named Fatima Santiago, but I've never seen her. I got locked up before she was born. Plus, I got a brother named Sammy, but everyone calls him Sam. His last name is Santiago. He's doing a small bid up at Leavenworth."

Once I heard him mention the name Sammy Santiago, my mind went blank. It was as if I was meeting the devil face-to-face. Tears rolled down my face, and anger took over my body. The only thing in my mind was avenging my grandfather's death. *Damn! There's no doubt in my mind that dis nigga next door is Fatima's father. I remember her telling me that her real father was serving a federal life sentence, but I don't remember her telling me about an uncle named Sam. Damn! What a muthafucking coincidence! Fuck it! What she don't know won't hurt her. Her loss is my gain.*

I needed to know more about this cat. "Old head, what did you say your brother's name was?"

"Sammy Santiago. His street name is Sam. Do you know him?"

"Nah, not really. The only Sammy I know is Sammy the Bull, and he's a rat! Oh, my bad! I do know that back in the day an old head from down my way named Sam killed a barbershop man down on Prospect Avenue, but he's locked up."

"Yo, man! That's him! That's my brother! He did only three and a half years for that case. He got out on good time. Once home, he started moving weight and got popped with a new case."

Santiago was too busy running his mouth to realize that I was picking his brain for information. "Old head, I need you to arrange it so that I could at least whip da Cuban boy's ass," I said, changing the topic of conversation.

"Young blood, I could do that for you. But if you're slow, you blow. That old nigga will get off on you if you let him. Believe me, he is not doing no fist fighting. Don't no one in this place who fist fights."

"Yeah, I feel you."

"Stick your hand through your cell bars," Santiago instructed me.

Once my hand was through the cell bars, he handed me a plastic shank made out of a food tray.

"Thanks, old head! I'll give it back to you when I'm done."

"Nah, you can have it. If you pull it out, use it. Handle your business. You'll have only three minutes to do what you gotta do. Six o'clock in the morning, the guard will crack two cells at a time for showers. If I don't sign up, you'll end up being put in the same shower stall with the Cuban boy. When they open your door, don't come out right away. Wait until the guard is back in the bubble. The Cuban boy always takes his time coming out of his cell. All you got to do is run up in his cell, do what you got to do, tuck his ass back in bed, and go take your shower. But make sure the guards see you going into the shower!"

The next morning, everything went as planned. As soon as the guard made his rounds for showers, Santiago didn't come out of his cell. The guard in the bubble who was monitoring the doors' control panel saw that he didn't open his door, so he hit my door open. I waited ten seconds, then ran up in the Cuban boy's cell and just took it to his ass. I caught the old nigga slipping, taking a shit with the cell door open.

"Talk dat shit now, *papi*!" I growled.

The Cuban boy never had a chance to defend himself, because the first stab wound I delivered to his chest put his lights out. It took less than a minute to send his old ass to hell.

As instructed, I tucked his ass back in his bed, with shit running down his legs, slammed his cell door shut, and went to take my shower. Once back in my cell, I broke the shank in half and flushed it down the toilet.

The old Cuban boy remained dead in his cell for four days before the other prisoners on the tier noticed that he hadn't been on the door, talking shit. Once the guards discovered that he was dead, they classified his death as a suicide. The entire tier was happy that his ass was dead.

A week later, I was notified by my caseworker that I was being transferred to Leavenworth Penitentiary. How lucky could a nigga be?

"Young blood, I see you're out of here tomorrow. When you get up there, make sure you get with my brother," Santiago said.

"I got you, old head! Just write him a kite, a note, and I'll make sure he gets it. Don't worry. I should be back on the streets soon. I promise that I'll find your daughter and mail you some pictures of her. I think I know who she is."

"Stop playing, young blood! You really think you know her?"

"Yeah, you faggot-ass nigga! I know who your daughter is! I've been fucking her in da ass every night for years now! The bitch knows how to suck a mean dick, and her pussy is something special. The next time I'm cumming up in her ass, I'm going to think of you! Oh, and your brother? As soon as I hit Leavenworth, I'm going to murder him! The barbershop man he killed was my grandfather! Don't worry. I'll make sure I give him your kite!" Those were my last words to Santiago.

When the guards woke me up at three in the morning to transfer me out, I stopped by Santiago's cell, and he was standing at the bars with a puppy dog look on his face. I spit dead in his face, and before he could react, the guards pushed me away from his cell, threw my ass on the floor, and shackled my legs and cuffed me up.

I was then escorted to a bus, which was to deliver me to the United States Penitentiary, Leavenworth, in Kansas City.

Chapter Nineteen

Revenge Is Always Sweeter

Rashad

Leavenworth Penitentiary . . .

Once again, I was placed in the hole. Although I was twenty-two years old, an adult by all rights, the prison officials felt that I was too young to be in Leavenworth. They didn't want to take the responsibility in the event anything happened to me. I wanted to be put out in general population. The other prisoners who arrived with me were more than happy to be put in the hole, because most of them were in exile from other federal prisons for ratting on other prisoners.

Two days later, I was seen by a prison review committee and was told the reason I was being placed in the hole.

"You came here as a prisoner with a reputation. And not a good one. Therefore, we decided to place you in solitary confinement," said the director who headed the committee.

I said nothing. I sat slumped in my chair at the long table, listening to these motherfuckas spew their bullshit.

"We've also determined that here in Leavenworth there may be some inmates who are looking to do you harm. You can stay in solitary and be safe, or you are free to go into general population, but we can't guarantee your safety."

"I ain't afraid of no one in here. Put me in general pop."

The director smiled. "As you wish."

They had me sign some papers stating I would not hold the federal prison system responsible in the event anything happened to me. And in answer to the question, "Where do you want your body sent in the event you die or get killed?" on one of the pages, I wrote, "Hell!" My frame of mind at this point was beyond gloomy.

I had heard stories of how violent Leavenworth was, but as a man, I couldn't let my fear dominate my decisions. I chose the life I was living, and I was prepared to live or die by the rules of the game. Prison was nothing more than another part of the game for me. Fuck dat! I wanted to step into the jungle, where death awaited.

Adapting to an environment like Leavenworth was easy for me. I knew how to maneuver among prisoners. I was not gonna let anything distract me from my mission. I was determined to destroy, hurt, or cripple anyone who stepped in my path or stepped to me saying the wrong shit out of their mouth.

Federal prisoners were content with their condition. They got caught up in the hype and the "luxuries": having good food, being able to walk around with twelve dollars' worth of quarters in their pockets, the vending machines on the housing unit, using the phones whenever they wanted to. These were the same niggas who claimed to be kingpins out in the world. Some of these niggas accepted their fate without fighting. Some became so comfortable with being locked up in a cell and fucking punks in the ass that they no longer called themselves men. To me, anyone wearing prison clothes was fair game.

From day one, I never forgot that I was just another muthafucka who shit, slept, and ate in the same place that two million other individuals did. But I refused to be broken.

Given that Leavenworth was one of the most dangerous penitentiaries in the United States of America, a place where they housed some of the most notorious criminals, people automatically assumed I was there for some major shit. By the end of my first day in general population, I had everything I needed, including a ten-inch-long shank with Sam's name on it.

Sam was an important figure at Leavenworth. He was one of the leaders of the notorious Puerto Rican street gang called the Ñetas. When I ran into him, he looked the same. I wanted to kill his ass on the spot, but instead, I played the role, making him feel like he was doing me a favor by taking me under his wing.

"Old head, I have a kite from your brother. He's good people. In fact, he told me to tell you that he's trying to get transferred down here," I told him.

"Young nigga, you look real familiar. Where're you from?" he asked me.

"I'm from Washington, D.C., but my mother lives up in the Bronx."

"Well, if you know my brother, then you are my people."

Me being one of the youngest prisoners there, I had to show I was able to hang with the big boys. The Ñetas gave me a set of their rules and inducted me into their organization, which meant I had to sustain an ass whipping from them for six minutes. No more, no less. I took it like a man.

The Ñetas had full control of all the activities involving the Hispanic population. Their reputation extended back to Puerto Rico, where in the early eighties, they perpetrated one of the bloodiest prison takeovers that Puerto Rico had ever seen. The Ñetas made it possible for all the young boys in Puerto Rico who were going into the prison system to do their time without having to worry about being raped by other inmates. They forced the penal system in Puerto Rico to separate out the *insectos*—rats, faggots, child rapists, booty bandits—and put them in the hole. If they labeled you an *insecto*, you were as good as dead. During the prison war in the Puerto Rican penal system, hundreds of *insectos* were killed, chopped into pieces, and flushed down the toilet.

Prison officials didn't know how to respond to the crisis. The Ñetas emerged as the victors and established themselves in every prison across the island of Puerto Rico, making it possible for anyone considered an *insecto* to live among real muthafuckas. Anyone who violated their rules had to die. The rules were as follows:

1. Respect your fellow prisoners at all times.
2. Do not steal from your fellow prisoners.
3. No fraternizing with the police, COs, or any employee of the prison.
4. Do not shower with, look at, touch, or try to force yourself on any homosexual.
5. Do not ask to be introduced to any other prisoner's family member.
6. Do not disrespect or inquire about someone else's visit.

7. Do not ever ask another prisoner to show
    you his family photos.
8. Be ready to participate in any and all activi-
    ties of the Ñetas organization, meaning that
    if you are called upon, you must be ready to
    arm yourself and do whatever is necessary.
9. Always keep the Ñetas' name in good stand-
    ing.
10. Violation of any or all of these rules will
    result in your death, with no mercy.

The Ñetas made it safe for some young niggas to
keep their assholes intact. They also made it safe
for niggas like Sam to hide his *insecto* ways. I was
prepared and willing to die, but Sam's days were
numbered.

The Ñetas summoned me to appear in front of
their committee, and I acted like it was an honor.
All the new Hispanics who arrived in Leavenworth
had to go through this process. It was the only
way a person could stay in general population.
The process was done to confirm your status as a
thoroughbred or an *insecto*. It began with a long
string of questions, and the person appearing in
front of the Ñetas' committee had to present his
intake papers, which clearly stated what you were
incarcerated for.

The voting was the most interesting part of the
process. The only way a person could become a

Ñeta was if he was voted in unanimously. All ten members of the committee had to vote. Six of the ten members had to vouch for you, and by doing so, they were putting their lives on the line, in the event that you turned out to be an *insecto*.

Out of the ten members on the committee, nine voted for me. The one who held back his vote was an old head named Cano, from Puerto Rico, who thought I was too young. But once he found out that I knew Sam's brother from Lewisburg, he gave me his vote.

Being a Ñeta in Leavenworth came with some jailhouse benefits. I was allowed to get my dick sucked and wet by a unit manager/caseworker whom the Ñetas had on their payroll. I was also allowed to use a smartphone to make outside calls. To me, none of that shit meant anything. Yeah, I won't front. Getting my dick sucked or wet in some pussy juice by this overweight Kansas City bitch was special, but my main mission was to murder Sam, so I stayed focused.

The more I looked at Sam, the more he resembled an alien from outer space. His dark complexion separated him from any other soul at Leavenworth. The scar that ran across his neck told me that he'd been in some serious drama in the past. His jaundiced eyes were the same eyes I had looked into the day he murdered my grandfather. They were always sparkling with lust. This bitch-ass nigga was an *insecto*. I boosted his ego by making him feel like he was looking out for me.

Then one night, while we were taking a shower, he stripped naked. I ignored him at first, but he was playing himself out.

"Rashad, real men take showers naked, feel me?" he said while stroking his dick.

"Nah, old head. I don't take showers naked unless I'm showering with my bitch," I told him while looking him straight in his eyes.

"There's no bitches in here. However, an asshole is an asshole. It don't matter if it's a man or a woman's asshole. I enjoy both," he said while still stroking his dick.

"I can't speak on dat, because I never had both."

"Why don't you try it, then?"

"Nah, I'm cool."

"Trust me, it feels the same, especially if you get a blow job before you tap the ass. If you ever want to try it, let me know. I'm known for giving an exceptional head job. Plus, by the print in your boxers, I can see you have a big fat dick. Just keep that in mind, and between us."

"I'll think about it, old head. I'll let you know tonight," I responded, letting him feel my dick through my boxers. It was unexpected, but my dick stood straight up when he touched it. I let him keep his hand there. We looked each other in the eyes. I wanted to kill him right then. Instead, I let him stroke my dick until I shot a fat load in his hand. He licked it up until it disappeared.

This nigga really thought that he was slick, but I had plans for him. This was his way of trying to turn me the fuck out, by letting me fuck him first. This was the oldest trick in prison. I'd seen this game before.

Right after the shower, rumors started making the rounds in the jail. Sam was telling mutha-fuckas that I was going to be his people. In prison language, that translated to I was going to be his punk fuck boy. Muthafuckas were waiting to see if my pretty ass was going to break and become a punk.

The Ñetas were behind this shit. Their jailhouse rules were nothing but a bunch of bullshit! These old dope-fiend niggas were a bunch of *insectos*! They thought I was sweet, but they never saw the raw nigga in me. I had to wait for a suitable time to seize the opportunity to strike when the iron was hot.

One afternoon I ran into Sam in the commissary line and decided to get this shit over with. "Sam, I thought about your advice, and I'm willing to try what we spoke about in the shower. I'm young, and I could release some stress. My fucking balls are hurting me. So, are you still willing?"

"Yeah! Yeah! Wait for me in the weight room. Remember, this is between you and me. Do you need anything from commissary?" he said.

"I'm cool. All I need is some ass."

"Look at you! I'll be there in a few," Sam said with a smile.

A half an hour later, I sat in the weight room, while everyone else was up in the game room, shooting pool, gambling, playing cards, or distributing the illegal drugs that made up the fabric of the institution.

Sam walked into the weight room with his shorts and a wife beater on, as if he was getting ready to conquer the world. "Rashad, I'm glad you decided to let me teach you a few things about prison life. Trust me, it's not as bad as it sounds. We'll both enjoy it."

Nigga, I don't know about you, but I know I'm gonna enjoy myself! Fuck yeah! I can't wait to see the look in your eyes when I stick this hot metal in your ass! "I'm not worried about anything, old head. I . . . I . . . I just never done dis before, but I trust you."

"Okay, let's lift a little bit of weight to loosen up."

Sam laid his six-foot-three-inch body on the weight bench, giving me an opportunity for a field day.

"Put five hundred pounds on this baby!" he ordered me as he leaned back and took hold of the weights.

When he lifted the weights off the rack, I took his habitual lack of awareness as an invitation to ruin his desire for sucking my dick. I pulled my shank out and butchered his faggot ass, stabbing him repeatedly in the chest and stomach. The weights came crashing down on him, crushing his chest. Blood poured out of his mouth like water from a water fountain.

"Sam, look at me, you fucking nut! Look at me! You never thought you would ever see me again, huh? But surprise! What a small world! You see, when you killed my grandfather and pointed your gun at me, you shoulda pulled the trigger! Remember me now?"

Damn! I shoulda killed that fucking kid! Ain't this a bitch! I hope he don't kill me. I'm not ready to die. Damn! These motherfucking weights are heavy! Sam thought to himself as the weights began rolling toward his neck.

"Dis is for my grandfather, pussy!" were the last words I said to Sam before chopping him down like the fucking pig that he was. His face frowned with agony, and his white teeth were now covered in blood. His screams brought out the animal gratification in me.

When the weights tilted off his neck, he rolled off the weight bench onto the floor. I stabbed him for the last time in his eyes, then plunged the shank deep into his heart. A smile came over my face as I watched my prey take his last breath. By then the weight room had a pungent scent of sweat and blood. It had the potential to turn your stomach inside out.

It felt miraculous to know that I had the power to reduce another nigga to nothing at any given time. Some muthafuckas in prison just didn't deserve the privilege to live, let alone be considered a human being. Sam was one of them.

Back in my cell, I strapped myself up by taping hardcover books around my upper body. The Ñetas wanted to move out on me, but they thought twice about it after they received the news that Sam had died. Instead, they dropped a slip under the deputy superintendent's office door that same night.

The next morning, the CERT team was at my cell door before the sun came up. I was placed under investigation, but two months later I was cleared, because they couldn't prove anything.

Sometimes we were forced to do things beyond our desires. I had come to prison with one intention, and that was to kill my brother for snitching on my mother. But along the way, this bitch-ass nigga Sam had popped up. What was I supposed to do? How lucky could a nigga get? He had had the chance to kill me and hadn't, so fuck him!

My philosophy was the same as Machiavelli's: I'd rather have a person fear me than respect me. When a muthafucka in prison feared you, he knew better than to step to you with some dumb shit unless he was willing to kill or be killed. Nowadays, there were very few niggas prepared to handle that kind of drama.

Fear was the only word that I had removed from my vocabulary, because without it, there was no doubt in my mind that I would survive this dehumanizing, physically cold, and harsh place. My quest was to be the only survivor left at the end of the game.

After the investigation into Sam's death was closed, I was snatched up in the middle of the night and transferred back to Pennsylvania, where I was turned over to the custody of the DOC official and was once again taken to Klan Hill Correctional Facility.

Chapter Twenty

Correctional Brutality

Rashad

The minute the blue bus arrived at Klan Hill, state troopers and prison officials surrounded it. My instincts told me to prepare for the ass whipping of my life, and I was right.

As soon as the bus door swung open, I was jumped on by an angry mob of correctional officers and state troopers. They carried me by my handcuffs and shackles into a room away from the other inmates, so that they couldn't see what was happening. I was forced to walk naked through a gauntlet of prison officers armed with billy clubs, gloved fists, and boots. They were trying to degrade me emotionally and torture me physically by subjecting me to these acts of brutality.

But no savage beast could break a real soldier. My head was busted open, my jaw was broken, and two of my ribs were cracked, and I still wouldn't give them the pleasure of hearing me beg them to stop.

After beating me for half an hour, they dragged me down the cellblock and threw me into a cell.

For a week straight, every time the shift changed, the guards would strap up in riot gear and come into my cell and beat me up. Other inmates suspected of participating in the riot were given the same treatment or worse.

After being in the hole for a month, I found out through another inmate that I was under investigation for sexually assaulting a guard. Now I understood why these clowns were on me the way they were! Some white boy named Patrick Rams had claimed that he saw me fucking a guard on April 26, when the riot first jumped off. Yeah, I was fucking that day, but it wasn't a guard! It was Fatima in the visiting room!

Prison officials knew that a case of that caliber against an inmate could generate a substantial amount of media attention, which could potentially make the prison officials shine brightly in the eyes of the public. Therefore, they were claiming that they had no record of anyone visiting me that day. But when Fatima got a lawyer, who produced the visitor's pass she was given on that day, they cleared me of any wrongdoing.

Society always bitched and moaned about justice, but for whom? The same society that sought out justice when I fucked up needed to stop being hypocritical when it was time to provide a nigga like me some justice. I had been falsely accused of sexually assaulting a prison guard, and all I had got was an ass whipping. Where the fuck was the justice in that?

So I sued Klan Hill for correctional brutality, false imprisonment, and the violation of my civil rights. We settled out of court for ninety thousand dollars and my immediate transfer to Heavenford Correctional Facility, which placed me within arm's reach of my brother.

I had eighty-five days until my max date.

Chapter Twenty-one

Nothing to Lose

Mustafa

Huntingdon State Prison in the mountain boon-docks of central Pennsylvania was run by white boys with vicious hard-ons for inner-city blacks and Hispanics.

CO Ski did not hesitate to express openly his dislike for me or anyone who was a Muslim. The first day I arrived, he began harassing me. I ignored him, because with the help that my nigga Rashad had given me, I had managed to convert my life sentence into six and a half to twelve years. I was really trying to make parole. Plus, Brenda had kept her word and was visiting a nigga once a month. I really wasn't in the zone to kill these crackas. Every time CO Ski saw me, he made it his business to say some smart shit to me.

"Cell two eighty-five, you got a visit!" CO Ski yelled.

I hopped up from my bunk. These were the best days in prison. There was a lot of time to do nothing. It got lonely and boring, but these visits kept me going. I left my cell, ready to see my baby.

When I got to the front desk to pick up my pass, CO Ski asked, "Boy, who the heck comes to visit you?"

I was feeling defiant. "None of your business, sir!"

"It's none of my business? Boy, you must not want your visit today. I'll tell you what. Since you got a smart mouth, why don't you take it back to your cell."

I stood there in disbelief.

"That's an order!" he shouted.

"What about my visit?"

"Your visit was just canceled!"

"*What?*"

"You heard me, nigger! Your visit has just been canceled!" He looked me in the eyes like I was supposed to be scared.

"I want to see a white shirt!" I demanded.

"Nigger, the only thing white you're going to be seeing is my face! Are you refusing to lock up?"

"Nah, I'm not refusing. I just want to know why you're canceling my visit." My dark glasses prevented him from looking into my eyes. He had no way of telling whether I was afraid of him, like the rest of the inmate population.

"I'm canceling your visit because I can! Because I don't like you, and because *I* run this place! Understand?"

I kept my composure. I wasn't about to ruin my chance to see my baby. "I still request to see a white shirt."

"I'm not going to tell you again. You have a direct order to take it back to your cell. After this, I will issue you a DC-one-forty-one—a misconduct!"

"You're right. You run this place. This is your house," I responded before walking back to my cell. I was mad, because Brenda had traveled damn near thirteen hours from the Bronx to come visit me. Sometimes a man had to do what he had to do. I figured if I wanted to see Brenda again, I'd have to swallow my pride and obey the officer, no matter how fucked up he was being.

I had a strong effect on CO Ski, which other inmates never had. Ever since he had caught his snow bunny getting fucked by a dark-skinned Puerto Rican, he had developed a deep hatred for Hispanics. And when I arrived at Huntingdon State Prison, he could have sworn that I looked like the nigga he had caught banging his snow bunny. Every time he looked at me, he must have seen visions of his wife getting hammered down by a long black dick.

Once in my cell, I packed all my personal property and legal work in my footlocker. I did some pushups and sit-ups, took a nap, and waited until the afternoon count was clear. All day I pondered whether I should give CO Ski a pass. I was desperate to let it go, but the little nigga in my head kept telling me, *Kill! Kill! Kill!* I couldn't let it go. I tried, but his disrespect was too much for me.

Since it was Friday, niggas would be heading out to *Jumah*, the Muslim service for prayer. It was the perfect time for me to fall back and test CO Ski's heart.

I wrapped a string around the handle of my shank and tied it up in my right hand. Then I got down on both knees and did *salah*. I needed the strength of Allah to help me through.

The inmates were heading to *Jumah* while I prayed. When I finished, I immediately walked to the front desk, where CO Ski sat, chewing tobacco and smiling. I just stared at him with pure hatred in my heart. *Kill! Kill! Kill! Kill him until he's dead!* rang in my head.

I took my dark glasses off, because I wanted him to see that I didn't fear him. I bent down below the desk, so he couldn't see me.

"Get up where I can see you," he commanded.

I stayed silent.

"You hear me?"

I needed to bait him to come out from behind the desk.

"You better get up where I can see you! You don't want me coming out there," he warned.

I remained crouched.

"All right, you're asking for an ass whupping." CO Ski came out from behind the desk.

CO Ski never saw the shank in my hand. Each blow drew blood in massive amounts. He tried to fight me off his ass by lying on his back and kicking his legs up wildly, which was the bullshit training they taught the guards. But I was too quick for him. Each blow brought an indescribable sound from him.

His punk-ass colleagues didn't intervene. They ran, instead.

"Get the fuck up, cracka! Cancel this!" I said, stabbing him in his neck.

CO Ski didn't want to die on the same prison floor where he had stomped defenseless human beings simply because of the color of their skin. "Oh my God! Don't let this nigger kill me!" he yelled.

His screams were heard throughout the prison, and just when I was about to deliver the last blow to his heart, a jailhouse informant named Billy No-Good jumped on my back and tried to play hero. I turned around and stabbed the shit out of him in his face. During this time, other guards dragged CO Ski to safety.

CO Ski was flown by helicopter to a nearby hospital, where he remained in critical condition for six weeks. Afterward, I was given a new case, which I ended up pleading guilty to. I received five to ten years, which would run together with my time. I basically got off.

My signature was engraved on CO Ski for life, because he would forever be shitting in a shit bag, which would remind him of the only Hispanic nigga in Huntingdon State Prison that he feared.

I ended up getting transferred down to Heavenford, to serve six months in the hole.

Chapter Twenty-two

Crooked-ford

Rashad

When I arrived at Heavenford, I detached myself from the rest of the prisoners. Once inside the intake room, I began to think of my mother. The intake room was filled with a bunch of parole violators telling their hood stories. Each face, no matter how torn up half of these niggas were, registered in my memory. Their hood stories, combined with their fitful bursts of laughter, belied the fucking danger lurking in the intake room. Booty bandits were observing the weak niggas in the room, making mental notes on whom they were going to rape.

Being back in Heavenford was like attaining my freedom. I was rebellious as fuck. I wanted to undermine the penal system for trying to set me up.

Prison officials at Klan Hill had thought they were punishing me by sending me back here, but in actuality, they had only done me a favor, and had officially issued my brother his death certificate.

Life meant nothing to most of the niggas at Heavenford. The "I don't give a fuck" mentality kept a nigga on his toes. Killers, rapists, burglars, baby rapists, dope dealers, scam artists, and all other kinds of criminally minded human beings on the face of the planet surrounded you daily. There was no guarantee that once you entered this place, you would leave it alive. Bitch-ass niggas didn't stand a chance of breathing the same air that thoroughbreds did. You either became a victim or the victimizer here. You were on your own. No friends or gangs would keep you alive. The only way to survive was to hone your instincts and become more vicious than the next convict or take protective custody.

I saw a familiar face staring at me, and a slow smile crept over his shaven face. I tried to ignore it, but I was starting to feel violated. Plus, the nigga was smacking his lips with a great deal of pleasure, not to mention he had lust in his eyes. I rose cautiously, walked closer to him, and then peered into the eyes of the chump who was gambling with his life.

"Damn, Rashad! For a minute I thought you was gonna act funny and shit toward me!"

"Nigga, you don't know me! I'll crack your fucking face open and kick your teeth out your mouth!"

Baby Love let his eyes travel down my body. There was something inquisitive about his eyes—something unpleasant. I could tell he was experiencing a chill deep in the core of his soul, where he rarely dared to look. I could tell by his body language that he was feeling intimidated and was wondering if I was going to unleash the terrible ass whipping he knew he had coming.

"Rashad, I'm sorry if you felt disrespected. I was just speaking and saying hi to a friend."

"Nah, nigga. You were looking at me as if you were sizing me up."

"No I wasn't. We both know I'm not cut out for no tough Tony shit. I know who you are and what you would do to me if I ever disrespected you. I know that not too many muthafuckas want to be seen speaking to a punk, but I'm a human being too."

I remained silent.

Baby Love went on. "So, now that we're clear, I'll make sure you end up in one of the housing units where all the action goes down," he said.

"What the fuck you mean, you're going to make sure I—"

"Lucky for you, I have some influence around here. Believe me, punks run this jail. Niggas trust me more than they trust their boys. I know who's doing what in here. I might be a punk boy, but in this place, I'm someone who makes shit happen." Suddenly, all fear died away from his face, as though swept away by an unseen hand.

Dis bitch-ass punk is running shit! I remember when he first got here. Look at him now. I got plans for him. I'm not bitter at him, I thought. "How much pull do you hold around here?"

"Put it this way. I know all the crooked guards. I know which female guards are fucking for money. I know who's bringing the drugs into the jail and who controls the underworld in here." He turned his head so he could look fully into my eyes, and a small smile built at the corners of his mouth.

"Once I get drugs in, I want to holla at you," I replied. "I could put more money than you ever seen on your commissary books. In fact, from now on, if anyone asks you about me, let them know that I'm your people."

To my surprise, Baby Love was considering my offer for a moment, and there was something like scorn on his face.

"I feel you on that, but your plans require me to be under your wing for a while," he finally said. "Nigga, I could get more drugs into dis place than any other nigga. Do you want to make money or not?" Baby Love felt like a kid in a candy store.

"Yeah!" I said.

"Dat's what I thought. You're going on D Block, where all the action in the jail goes down. Plus, I'ma make sure you stay in a cell by yourself," Baby Love whispered.

"What block are you on?"

"D Block."

"Good."

"Good? Rashad, you know people are going to think that you're fucking me if they see me under your wing."

"Let me deal with dat."

After observing who was who and who was running what in the jail, I personally decided to recruit a young nigga who went by the name of Hot Karate. I had seen him on *America's Most Wanted* a week prior to meeting him. On TV he looked as if he was six feet five, but in real live, he was five-five, light skinned, with a vicious hate for rats and snitches. He knew who I was from reading the *Don Diva* magazine and from hearing jailhouse war stories about me from other inmates. We ended up being walkies, working out together and scheming over the fabric of the society called "the house of justice."

"Rashad, this place is only good for three things. Making money by pushing weight in here, becoming a better criminal, and corrupting those who society hires to watch over us. Half of these bitches will fuck and suck for a few dollars. I'm broke. Why don't you help a nigga get on his feet?" Hot Karate said. He was in a diabolical quandary.

"Nigga, I told you that I'm not trying to get caught up in no dumb shit. I'm getting ready to bounce in a minute. But I'll tell you what. If you can find yourself someone who will bring you a package, I'll give you enough dope to raise lawyer money."

"Bet! I could work with that."

I had Fatima FedEx Hot Karate's wife a fifth of a brick of pure heroin. Within a week, he had the entire jail on lock. Dope fiend–ass niggas were all overdosing by the dozens. Female guards were giving up the pussy to Hot Karate with the snap of his fingers. The top-level officials knew what was going on, but since Hot Karate kept their pockets full of money, they looked the other way. They weren't gonna jeopardize their extra cash. Everyone was eating healthy.

Most of the stabbings, rapes, murders, extortions, and assaults that took place in here were fueled by the guards. It was the norm for them to set other inmates up for the kill. Most of the guards in Heavenford had no shame in offering their services for a price.

Hot Karate had a bitch named Ms. Trenton, and she would bring him his package straight to his cell. This bitch was known throughout the jail for being a smut and a freak bitch, whose main source of income was fucking the white guards for their paychecks.

Two weeks later . . .

As I was returning from the main yard, I noticed a group of inmates in orange jumpsuits. On Thursdays, niggas were released from the RHU, the hole. I was walking past the group of niggas, who were lined up, waiting to be assigned a cell, when I heard my name.

"Rashad!"

I lifted my head so I could see the figure in the orange jumpsuit. I walked up to him and gave him a brotherly hug.

"Damn, Mustafa! When did you get here?" I asked him.

"B, I been in the hole for the past six months. I caught a new charge for serving a guard. I got five to ten, running wild with my time. I'm glad to see you, bro!"

"Fatima told me you gave your time back!"

"Yeah. Thanks to you, a nigga will see the streets again. I see parole in a few months, but we both know them crackas gonna give a nigga a hit from the door."

"Nigga, the bottom line is that you will be out. Me, I got less than ninety days to max. By the way, what's up with you and Brenda?"

"Baby girl been riding with me hard."

"Just don't fall in love with a bitch. She's a hood rat who stays on the grind."

"I hear you, B," Mustafa said, then nodded in agreement.

"What cell they assigned you to?"

"I don't know yet."

"Fuck dat! You're going in my cell," I responded as I walked away from him. I headed over to speak with Baby Love, who was in the unit manager's office, assigning cells. Once I explained to him that my people was on the block, he assigned Mustafa to my cell. I went back to where Mustafa was standing.

"Nigga, you're going to my cell," I told him.

He just shook his head and followed me to the cell.

"B, I see you have a little juice around here," he commented when we reached my cell.

"Nigga, whatever is in this cell is yours."

That same day . . .

She walked with a seductive rhythm. Her lusty big brown eyes had money written all over them. Her chocolate-brown skin made her resemble an African queen. Her big ass was like a bowl of Jell-O, which had niggas on D Block running to their cells, throwing their door curtains up, and taking care of their fantasies.

Ms. Trenton knew that pussy-hungry niggas on the cellblock loved watching her walk up and down the tier. The bitch had a fan club of niggas, who cooked jailhouse-made food for her just to be seen next to her. She made it her business to shake her big ass a little extra when she saw me. I paid the bitch no mind. Rumors around the jail were that she was a swallowing kind of chick. The bitch was dirty. She was irrelevant, and in my opinion, she didn't even exist.

"Rashad, I need a load. You know my money's good, man. So look out for your old head," Fat Man said with a hoarse voice.

Fat Man was the biggest rat in the jail. He worked for the security office at the institution. He was one of those old niggas who had been in jail for thirty-seven years, doing nothing but playing softball and ratting on niggas. He knew when new policies were coming out even before the rest of the population knew about them. He was a boot-licking Uncle Tom nigger that didn't have a problem dropping a dime on anyone. If a muthafucka wasn't willing to kill him, it was best to leave him alone.

"Fat Man, it depends on how much we're talking about."

"Man, fuck the money! I need you to holla at your young boy, Hot Karate, so he can give me a few bags of that shit he got," he said with a stern look.

I reached into my pants pocket and pulled out a one-hundred-dollar bill. "Fat Man, I don't interfere with another nigga's hustle. But why don't you take this hundred dollars and go cop yourself three bags?"

"Man, you know how Hot Karate be acting. If he sees me, he won't sell me any."

"Then you're out of luck, because I'm not gonna cop for you."

"Young buck, if you do this for me, I'll bless you with something nice," Fat Man said as he reached into his back pocket and pulled out an envelope.

Dis snitch-ass dope fiend makes me sick! I'm willing to bet he would suck a dick for a bag of dope. I don't understand how a nigga can degrade himself for a bag of dope, I thought to myself as I observed him pulling a stack of naked pictures out of the envelope. I could see that he was desperate, with a gorilla on his back, so I held the hundred-dollar bill tightly in my hand. I was determined to make him suffer a li'l bit.

He began flipping through the pictures. My eyes grew wider. I wanted to snatch them out of his hand, but I remained cool. If I showed any interest, this dope-fiend snitch nigga might up his price. "Listen here, old head. I'ma go ahead and give you three of my bags, but don't come back!" I said as I snatched the envelope out of his hand.

"Okay."

"Turn your back," I said. Didn't want this snitch bitch seeing where I stashed my dope.

I reached under my bunk and removed the false front to the wall. It was a piece about four inches wide and six inches high. Inside the wall, I had carved a hole big enough for my paraphernalia: my shank, some dope packets, and whatever else that needed to be hidden. I removed three packets and gave them to Fat Man.

"Good lookin', Rashad. I won't forget this."

Once Fat Man was out of my cell, Mustafa and I viewed each picture carefully. "Nigga, I'm about to fuck this little whore down with these!" I said to Mustafa, who was lying on his bunk bed and observing me.

"B, that whore is nothing but a smut. She's trash."

"Yeah, I know, but the flip side is that she would move out for a nigga for the right price. It's worth a try."

"I got your back," Mustafa said as we heard the distant roaring of pussy-hungry convicts. He sat up in bed and smiled, anticipating my next move. We could hear keys jingling and niggas making all kinds of dirty remarks.

"Damn! That whore ain't got no panties on!" one inmate yelled.

"I would love to eat her pussy!" another one said and licked his lips.

"You two old niggas are the wrong color. That whore only fucks with white boys," a young inmate said as Ms. Trenton approached his cell.

"You can't hang out on the tier," she said and gave the young nigga a direct order to get off the tier.

When she made her way toward my cell and stood in front of my door, I gave her a serious stare. "How you doing today, Rashad?" she asked me nonchalantly.

"I don't know about my cellmate, but I'm stressed da fuck out," I responded tersely.

"After I'm done making my rounds, I'll be in the unit manager's office. If you want to talk about what it is that you're stressing about, I'll be there," Ms. Trenton said flatly, then continued doing her rounds and shaking her fat ass a li'l extra.

I smiled at Mustafa, who was lying on his bunk and acting as if he wasn't ear hustling. "B, I don't trust that whore," he said.

"Neither do I, but I'm about to test her game. There are only two things she could do to me—write me da fuck up and take me to the hole or play da game and make some money. I'm willing to bet she's gonna play da game."

"We'll see."

"Yeah. If I'm not back from the unit manager's office in an hour, then you know I'm booked. All I need is for you to look out and make sure no unwanted nigga walks in on me."

"I got your back, B."

Money was power, and power was money in Heavenford. When prison guards came to work for eight hours a day and witnessed a convict banking in more money than the guards made in two weeks of work, they started questioning their oath toward their job and whether they should be a part of the profitable prison system. They thought, *Why put my life in danger for a paycheck when I can make twice as much by looking the other way?*

A lot of the female guards who worked in corrections didn't get the attention on the streets that they received in here. Ninety percent of them were welfare recipients, with no formal education whatsoever. It didn't take much to turn a key and lock up a nigga's ass.

These whores who came to work here were torn the fuck up from head to toe and looked like zombies. But as soon as they received their first paycheck, they would run to the Chinese store to buy fake hair, nails, and contact lenses. Then they would come back to work with fake attitudes, like their shit didn't stink, and acting all law and order.

Ms. Trenton was no different. She was one of those hating-ass bitches who fucked with people's families out in the visiting area when they came to visit. She was so dirty that she would make our families wait for two to three hours before allowing them into the visiting room. The bitch forgot that she had come out of the same gutter most of us in here were from, so every chance I got to do one of those bitches dirty, it was on and popping.

Bitches like Ms. Trenton were known as "bloodsuckers." In fact, she was the ringleader of the infamous crew called the Pussy Pound Girls, which was a crew of Black and Hispanic female correctional officers who sold pussy to the white guards.

Anything a nigga wished for in prison was made available to him in Heavenford. The Pussy Pound Girls didn't discriminate. If a nigga was getting some major paper in here, they were on his heels. Sex for money on a daily basis was the order of the day. For two hundred dollars, a nigga could get the pleasure of feeling some burning lips wrap around his dick. For five hundred, he could get a trip around the world, consisting of a shot of ass and some pussy. There was no greater feeling than that of corrupting the morals of these society heads watching over me.

The chapel, the school building, the infirmary, the supply rooms, the major's office, and the unit manager's office were the prime tricking spots in the jail. It wasn't unusual to see a female guard getting her back blown out while bent over a desk. Sergeants, lieutenants, captains, schoolteachers, and shop supervisors were all part of the underworld in Heavenford.

The unit manager's office, D Block . . .

When I walked into the unit manager's office, Ms. Trenton was sitting behind the desk, as if it was her own. "So, tell me, Rashad, why a cute nigga like you is stressing," she said.

"Ms. Trenton, I just said dat because I didn't want my cellmate to be up in my business."

"Oh, so you're one of those niggas that just want some conversation, huh?"

"You got me confused with these Philly niggas. Do I look lonely? I just wanted to pull your coat on something," I said and pulled Fat Man's envelope out of my back pocket and laid the pictures one at a time on top of the desk. I could see her trying to develop her next sentence within the chambers of her slow mind.

"Where did you get those from?" she asked once she had got her thoughts together.

"Do I look like a Philly nigga to you? What matters is that I'm returning them to you."

"Did you look at them? I bet that you probably beat your dick off them."

"Nah. I'd rather have the real thing. Plus, I got less than ninety days to max out."

"I know. I already looked you up on the computer."

"So, then you know my history and what I'm about."

"Get to the point."

"These pictures in the hands of Philly niggas can make you a public commodity. But I'm not into blackmailing anyone. I pay for what I want."

"The price of pussy in here ain't cheap."

"If a nigga's got to ask how much, it seems that he can't afford it," I replied as she got up from behind the unit manager's desk and locked the door from the inside.

She dropped to her knees in front of me and asked, "So, I'm guessing you want some head?"

"Nah. I want a trip around the world. I want the whole package."

She unzipped her dark blue correctional officer's pants and dropped them to her ankles. Then she took her shirt off. Watching this dirty whore standing in front of me, butt ass naked, was driving me crazy. With the inbred morals of a whore, she unzipped my pants and stared at my dick, with her mouth slightly open.

Man! This nigga's dick is triple the size of any of the white boy guards I been fucking! I'ma juice this nigga for every dollar he's got on his books, she thought.

She scooped my balls into her palms, opened her mouth wide, let her lips caress my thick shaft, and then allowed my dick to slide in and out of her wet mouth. With only seven inches of my dick in her mouth, she could feel it touching the back of her throat. "Mmmm!" she let out, loving the taste of my dick and loving the way my balls banged into her chin on every downbeat.

I hope I can take the entire dick in my mouth, she thought.

After letting this whore get used to my dick, I felt it was time to do her dirty. Now, that was what I call excitement!

"Deep throat me, bitch! I wanna cum down your hot throat!" I said as I gripped her head tightly and rammed my dick down her throat. I held her head tightly until my cum was spurting out of my dick and coating her lips and throat and dribbling from the corners of her mouth. She gasped and tried to pull her head back, but my grip was too tight for her to break loose.

Once I was finished cumming down her throat, I clutched her chin and lifted my dick and let it rest on top of her nose while I placed my balls inside her mouth. "Suck 'em! Make my dick hard again! Play with your pussy while you're sucking my balls."

"Let me suck you off."

"Bitch, I'm running this show! But since you want to suck, I'll let you suck," I said with a smile. I had every intention of making this whore earn her money. It was only a matter of time before she was trying to back away from the dick, but I held her tightly.

Damn! My lips hurt and my jaw aches. I have never in my life seen a dick this big. Mmmm! she thought.

She began to finger fuck herself to the point where she wanted some dick up in her. Just when she was really getting into it, I gripped her head and guided her moist lips on and off my dick. She thought she was going to choke when I pushed her head down until my balls were banging against her chin. She tried to hold back, but the pressure in the back of her throat was too much, and she puked all over my dick while I unloaded a load of cum onto her stomach.

"What the fuck!" I exclaimed.

"I'm sorry!"

"Sorry? Bitch, since you want to get nasty, climb your ass on that desk, so I can get a taste of that ass. I'ma show you how nasty a nigga can get!"

"Nigga, we ain't got a lot of time. I can't be up in this office for too long, so you got to wet your dick and pull out."

"Stop rapping and get your fat ass on that desk!"

Once she was lying on top of the desk, on her back, I took both of her legs and pressed her knees up against her chest, exposing her fat pussy and asshole.

"Put it in me!" Ms. Trenton let out in a soft, thin voice.

"You forgot who's paying who. I'm taking my time," I said as I rammed my dick into her pussy to the hilt.

Damn! This bitch is gutted! She ain't got no walls! I thought to myself as I contemplated my next move. I made sure my dick was nice and wet before I decided to show this whore how dirty a nigga could get. Without warning, I pulled out of her and stuck my dick into her asshole. She tensed instinctively, which turned me on.

"Take it out now!" she whispered.

I paid the bitch no mind. The tenser she became, the harder I pushed into her asshole. "I'm going to cum in your ass now! Damn! Keep it tight for me! Ooh, yes!"

Ms. Trenton almost fainted from the pain and pleasure as my tempo increased. I penetrated her asshole as deeply as possible. She shivered with animal pleasure as I unloaded my load deep in her. When I pulled out of her, I let my dick rest on her pussy lips. I grabbed the unit manager's sweater, which was lying on a chair, and wiped my dick and nuts clean. Then I reached into my back pocket and pulled out a bankroll of hundred-dollar bills. Before Ms. Trenton could fully recover from her orgasm, I started inserting hundred-dollar bills into her leaking asshole. By the time she recovered, she had ten one-hundred-dollar bills halfway in her busted booty.

"You son of a bitch! Why would you do some shit like that?" she snarled.

"Whore, you just made one thousand for doing something you love to do. Fucking!" I said with a smile.

"Fuck you and your shitty-ass money!"

"Look at it this way. How many bitches in this place can say they had some dead presidents up their ass?"

"Oh, now you got jokes!"

"Ms. Trenton, I got another five thousand dollars in cash . . . if you do me a favor."

The word *cash* brought the bitch back to reality. She got off the desk and stuffed her nasty ass back into her correctional officer's uniform without cleaning herself. The whole office smelled like ass. "It depends on what favor you want," she said.

"Nothing big."

"I'm listening."

"My li'l brother is in lockup down on J Block, and he's supposed to be going home soon. We haven't seen each other for years. As stated, I have five grand if you can get him out of the hole."

"What's his name and institution number?"

"Flash Lopez, CJ-two-two-eight-nine," I replied as she started playing with the unit manager's computer.

Within three minutes, she had Flash's picture and record up on the screen. "Yo, your brother is signing out next week. His max date is next Tuesday. Let me see what I can do."

She picked up the phone and called J Block. "LT, who's standing around?" she asked and licked her lips. "Cool! I need a favor. An inmate by the name of Flash Lopez, can you release him to D Block . . . ? Nigga, don't I always take care of you? Put it this way. Make it happen today and I'll bless you with a thousand dollars cash . . . Yeah, okay, I'll do that now," Ms. Trenton said with a smile and began to type up a request to release Flash from the hole under the major of the guards' name.

"What up?"

"Nigga, your brother will be out of the hole in about a half hour. I'm telling you now, I don't know how he got out of the hole, if anyone asks," she said with a concerned look.

"Do I look like a Philly nigga to you?" I asked as I pulled out another bankroll from my back pocket and handed it to her. Then I added, "By the way, when he gets to the block, put him in Baby Love's cell."

J Block, Heavenford Prison, the hole . . .

Officer Davis stood in front of inmate Flash Lopez's cell and issued an order. "Mr. Lopez, pack your things up. You're going to population, D Block! Speed it up! You got to be on top before count!"

"What? You must be mistaken," Flash replied nervously.

"No, sir, I'm not mistaken."

"But—"

"I'm in no fucking mood for your shit! Pack your shit up now, or you'll lose it!"

"Can I see a white shirt?" Flash asked with a touch of pride.

"You can see a white shirt when you get up top."

Flash Lopez obeyed and packed his things. *Fuck it! I got only a week left before I get out of this place. It can't be that bad up top*, he told himself silently.

"You ready, Mr. Lopez?" Officer Davis asked angrily, because she had been thrown into the mix of some dumb shit. On the surface, there was nothing strange about an inmate being released from protective custody, and yet, it was strange . . .

very strange, because most inmates in protective custody could be released from the hole only by the PRC, the Prison Review Committee.

Thirty-five minutes later . . .

I stood by the radiator with my baseball cap down to my eyes, observing my brother, Li'l Flash, in an orange jumpsuit as he stood by Ms. Trenton, looking bewildered and staring down the cellblock with his head hung low. The second he stepped onto D Block and was thrown to the wolves, he ceased to exist. He seemed to look at nobody. When Ms. Trenton led him to his cell, a smile crept over my shaven face.

That same night . . .

After the four o'clock count was clear, Baby Love rushed out of his cell and reported to work. I waited until the section officer hit the levers to open the doors for chow. When it was clear, I made my way down to Baby Love's cell, a piece of metal pipe stuffed up my sleeve. The door was closed, and to my luck, a sheet was up for privacy. I couldn't have planned it any better. My brother had no idea how much he had helped me. He was making it easy for me to achieve my goal.

I stood in front of Baby Love's cell for two minutes before I opened the door. My body was humming with anticipation. It had been a long road to this destination, and I had finally got here. I'd done a lot of shit and put up with even more. Revenge was about to be mine.

I stepped behind the sheet. Flash was sitting on the toilet, taking a shit. The element of surprise made his body shake with fear, and his eyes glazed over with tears.

"Rashad!"

"It's me, nigga."

"How did you get in here?"

"I walked in, nigga. I been putting my time in, making moves in order to get transferred here. You're snitch ass is about to pay."

"Forgive me!" he whispered hoarsely.

"Forgive you!" I smiled. This rat-ass punk was trippin'.

Flash couldn't believe his eyes. He was undecided about whether to get up from the toilet and wipe his ass clean or remain seated. "Rashad, I didn't testify against you, man!"

"But you were going to, if given the chance! Your statement gave the prosecutor leeway!"

"No, no. Listen."

I swung the piece of metal pipe down and shattered the top of his skull. Flash's eyes rolled up in his head. He fell to the floor with his ass up in the air and lay there in a pool of blood. I nudged him with my foot. He was limp.

"See you in hell, snitch-ass bitch."

I took Baby Love's bedsheet and tied one end to the radiator in the cell. Flash's dead weight was harder to move than I had thought it would be. I dragged him over to the radiator and fashioned a noose with the bedsheet and tied it around his neck. I pulled the sheet until he was hanging from the radiator.

I peeked out from behind the sheet to make sure the tier was empty. With no time to waste, I leaped out of the cell and headed toward the chow hall to join the rest of the inmates. I ate my meal like I normally did, as all the other inmates went about their shitty lives none the wiser. My goal was accomplished. Now I just had to ride out the rest of my bid, and I'd be back out and running my kingpin game again.

Chapter Twenty-three

Man Down

Rashad

Baby Love was still in the chow hall and was unaware of the shitty dead nigga that was hanging in his cell. In fact, no one on D Block had noticed yet, because there was a sheet up at Baby Love's cell door, which meant that he was either using the toilet or handling his business. Niggas on D Block went about their normal routine. With over five hundred inmates on the grind, no one suspected that a snitch-ass nigga was getting ready to stink the place up.

Every other nigga in Heavenford was here because some hot-ass nigga had dropped dime on them. Some people might think that I was fucking crazy for fulfilling a promise I had made to myself. But yo, why should I let my brother live when he was willing and able to testify against the woman who had given him life? Why should he enjoy life when my mother had been given a life sentence, which equaled death by incarceration? On top of that, she had lost a leg.

The life I chose to live was not for cowards. They said that blood was thicker than water, and it might be so. Nevertheless, I lived by the cold of the streets. The game loved no one, and Flash shoulda known that. Since he had violated and betrayed his own blood, he had been rewarded with the ultimate gift that could be bestowed upon a hot nigga. *Death!*

Nine o'clock that night . . .

When the officer's voice on D Block came over the horn and announced lockup time, I stood by my cell door, looking toward Baby Love's cell. The muscles in my body were tense.

It won't be long now. Baby Love is in for a surprise. I just want to see his facial expression when he walks into his cell. Oh shit! Here he comes! I thought to myself as I watched him approach the front of his cell.

"Cellie! Cellie, are you using the toilet?" Baby Love asked through the crack in his cell door, but he got no response. *Fuck! That nigga's got to get out of my cell. There's only room for one queen in that cell*, he thought as the guard stood in front of him and banged on the cell door with a clipboard that held the count sheet.

"Take that sheet down! Count time!" another guard yelled.

"Don't make me open this door!" the guard with the clipboard said as he stuck his key into the hole and pushed the door wide open. "Oh, shit! God damn it!" he yelled. He dropped the clipboard and ran down the cell block, yelling, "Man down! Man down!"

The scent of blood and shit infused the cellblock. I couldn't help inhaling the smell of my brother's rotten body into my lungs.

Flash's body remained hanging in Baby Love's cell until the state police came in to investigate. At a quarter to ten, the same guard who had made the gruesome discovery was ordered by the superintendent to cut the sheet, take the body down to the medical department, and keep it there until the medical examiner arrived to transport it to the morgue.

"Hey, asshole! Before you take him to medical, make sure you cuff him up. He's not officially dead until the state police run his fingerprints through the EU database. Be quick! I'm trying to be out of here by ten o'clock!" the superintendent ordered and then walked away with a smile.

"Suicide. I guess some assholes can't do the time," one of the guards said.

"Yeah. If you can't do the time, don't do the crime . . . Don't do it!" the other guards sang with smiles on their faces. To them, a dead inmate was nothing but trash.

The next morning . . .

The next morning, the prison gossips were out in general population, spreading stories on what they thought had happened.

"I'm telling you, Baby Love did it," a nigga named Big Shame said to a female guard who was trying to hustle a pack of Newports from him.

"Nah. That punk don't have the balls to do no shit like that," said an inmate named Take.

"Both of y'all niggas are worse than bitches! I really don't care who did it, as long as it didn't happen on my watch!" said the fat, dark-skinned guard, who looked like she had eaten too many jailhouse meals, after the ass-kissing nigga gave her a pack of Newports. "Y'all two niggas give all the real niggas in this place a bad name. Niggas like y'all are the reason why a bitch can't do shit. Y'all talk too much!" she continued.

"Oh yeah?" Take said with a smile.

"Stop playing, Ms. Peters!" Big Shame said.

"*Playing*? Do I look like I'm playing? I get to go home every day at two fifteen, and believe me, nigga, neither one of y'all two niggas are on my mind." Ms. Peters's nasty-looking ass was deriving much enjoyment in putting these two clowns on blast.

I stood by my cell door, enjoying the spectacle that the out-of-shape whore was making of herself. Suddenly, Ms. Trenton walked by and leveled a murderous stare at me and received a wink in return. She shook her head and refocused on her surroundings. I waited a few minutes, until she had made her way to the unit manager's office, before I decided to put the finishing touches on my plans.

The second I entered the office, Ms. Trenton went off. "You put my job at risk!"

"I don't know what you're talking about! You had a choice in the matter, and you chose to take the five thousand dollars, right?"

"But—"

"But, my ass! Nothing else matters to me."

"But it doesn't make sense. I thought he—"

"You thought wrong! You didn't get paid to think!"

"Why did you lie?" she asked. Her eyes were large and glistening with anger.

"Because I don't trust the police."

"Oh, now I'm the police?"

"Bitch, you been the police from day one! Now, you can stand there running your mouth, or you can drop your pants down to your ankles so I can wet my dick!"

Ms. Trenton looked at me with a frown. "Nigga, you're lucky I kinda like you," she said.

"I kinda like you too. Now, drop your pants. I'm horny as hell," I said as I pulled my dick out and placed it in her hand.

"It's too early for this shit."

"Bitch, do you want to make this money or what?"

"How much are we talking about?" she asked.

"How much you need?"

"Well, I got the car payment coming up—"

"I ain't trying to hear all that shit. How much you need?"

"About a grand."

I reached into my pocket and pulled out a stack of bills. After I counted out a grand, I handed the bills to her and then said, "Drop your panties, *puta negra*!"

"Why do niggas in prison always want to fuck a bitch in the ass?" she asked. Her eyes sparkled with conviction.

"Because most of y'all whores' pussies are tore the fuck up. No disrespect, but I can't really do shit with your pussy, and I got a big dick!"

"This is all a game to you, isn't it?"

"Ain't that the same game you're playing? Keep it one hundred! Would I be here fucking you in the ass if I didn't have any money?"

"Whatever, nigga! Come on. Give me some dick."

Ms. Trenton bent over the unit manager's desk and dropped her panties to her ankles. I stood behind her and cracked her ass cheeks open with my right hand. For a second, I was tempted to wet my dick in her pussy, but why should I give her a pass? An easy fuck? Fuck her! I wanted this bitch to feel some pain!

"Let me suck your dick first," she said, looking over her shoulder. She wiped the perspiration off her sucking lips with her tongue.

"Nah, I'm cool," I responded, and then I penetrated her asshole with a violent thrust. I went in ball deep with one thrust and busted her asshole open. I felt the warm blood dripping down the side of my dick.

"God damn it! Take it out!" Ms. Trenton whispered through clenched teeth.

I gripped her waist and pulled all the way out, then penetrated her again. I repeated the process over and over until I felt my balls tighten. When I pulled out of her for the final time, I unloaded my cum all over the crack of her ass and her back. "Now you can suck my dick if you want!" I said to her.

"You are a freaky nigga!"

"Bitch, why don't you shut the fuck up! You are about to fuck up my mood. Just suck my dick clean," I said as I pulled five one-hundred-dollar bills from my pocket and threw them on top of the desk. *I bet this will motivate this whore to suck my dick!*

"Man, you're lucky I got my car payment due," Ms. Trenton said and began to lick my balls and dick clean.

Every nigga in prison loved a dirty whore. Ms. Trenton was every nigga on D Block's dream, and every tax-paying citizen's nightmare.

"Get it all!" I ordered.

"Are you serious? The last time I tried to deep throat you, I almost choked!" she said as she licked the head of my dick.

"Who the fuck taught you how to suck? You gotta have the best head game in this place." *Damn! This nasty whore has me ready to come again!* I thought as I shot hot cum all over her face.

She got up off her knees and grabbed a handful of tissues from the desk and put the wad against her asshole. "I think there's some internal bleeding!" she said while wiping her face.

"You'll be all right. I'm about to get me something to eat. I'm hungry as a muthafucka!"

"Hook a sista up with something to eat?"

"I got you, Ma. I got to keep you healthy. I love the freak in you. If I was home, you would definitely be wifey!" The lie rolled easily off my lips.

"You're supposed to be out of here soon, right?"

"In a hot minute."

"Maybe we can hook up."

"Only if you keep that ass popping the way you do!"

"You already know how I get down!"

This whore must have bumped her fucking head somewhere. Wifey! I wouldn't give this whore a penny if I was on the bricks! "We'll talk when the time is right. But if you're gonna be wifey, then the ass comes for free. I'll be back in five minutes. My man down in the kitchen is waiting on me with some home-cooked food."

When I returned to the unit manager's office with a hot pizza bagel and a bottle of iced tea, Ms. Trenton was all smiles.

Yeah, I got this little nigga whipped. I bet he thinks he got me turned out. I just want to see his expression when I give him back his money. I can get more out of him. He's got enough money to keep a bitch living good, Ms. Trenton thought to herself as she wrapped her lips around the bottle of iced tea.

"Here you go, Rashad," she said and placed the money that I had given her in my hands.

If this bitch wants to give me my bread back, fuck it! I'm taking it! I thought. "Nah, you earned that," I said, looking into her eyes. I saw right through her dirty ass. *Bitch, I'm playing your game!*

"Your dick is too good for me to be charging you. I only charge niggas that can't handle the ass."

"At least I made the ass bleed!"

"I know that's right!" she responded.

I put the money back in my pocket and bounced.

A half hour later . . .

"Yo, B! What the fuck is going on over there?" Mustafa asked as we were returning from the yard. He was pointing toward the unit manager's office, where a group of correctional officers was standing around while an institutional nurse performed CPR on a guard who was sprawled out on the floor.

"Keep it moving, fellows!" one guard yelled as the inmates returning from the yard began to gather around to try to get a glimpse of the guard on the floor.

"Fuck that bitch! Let her die!" one angry inmate said as he walked by.

"Yeah, she wasn't shit anyway!" another inmate said.

I kept walking toward my cell, as if nothing was happening. As far as I was concerned, the antifreeze had done what it was supposed to do. Thanks to Tru TV and the episode it had run on how to kill someone without using deadly force, I got to solve a problem without even getting my hands dirty.

Ms. Trenton was DOA by the time she was taken to an outside hospital. No one at Heavenford was able to unravel the mystery of her death. Heart failure was listed as the cause of death, according to the official report the Pennsylvania Department of Corrections put out to the general public.

Baby Love was let out of the hole two days later, only to overdose on a bag of dope that he had purchased from Hot Karate.

Mustafa never found out that the punk, hot nigga who was murdered in Baby Love's cell was my brother.

What happened two days ago in the unit manager's office, no one would ever know who did it . . . at least no one who was alive!

Chapter Twenty-four

One More Chance

Rashad

I should have been grateful that I was going home today, but I wasn't. I had come to prison with a purpose, and I had done what I had said I was going to do. I had no regrets about my time spent there.

It was 6:25 a.m. I got up from my bunk bed for the last time, washed my face, threw on my prison browns for the last time, and waited for the punk-ass guard to open my cell door.

Normally at Heavenford—or at any other state correctional facility—they tried to release you before the rest of the population was let out of their cells. The reason for this was that there were some nut-ass niggas in here who specialized in fucking other people's time up. They waited until someone was going home to stab him or to start some dumb shit. If a nigga wasn't maxing out and he got into some dumb shit, his parole was revoked on the spot.

This particular day I did something I had never done during all the time I'd been in this place. I looked out the window. The day was lovely. The temperature was in the eighties, the sun was shining, and there was no wind. Like Ice Cube said, "It was a good day!"

"This is your chance, nigga, to get rid of all the nonsense that's clattering around in your head. Now is the time to leave all this prison shit in here. This is your chance to grow up," Mustafa said, giving me a cold stare as we stood face-to-face in the cell.

"What?"

"You need to understand how lucky we are. We're getting another chance at life. The second you walk out of this place, you will be on your goddamned own. I do you no favor if I let you think you're not."

"Nigga, I got a loyal team with me."

"Yo, B! That might be the case, but at the end of the day, the only thing you have is your courage and intelligence."

"Nigga, just make sure you call me every day. I'ma JPay you money every other day. Bro, I'm really grateful that I had the opportunity to break bread with you," I said with a trembling voice.

"Likewise, my nigga! It was a pleasure."

"Mustafa, this place makes the whole world seem ugly."

"It gets better on the other side of the wall."

When CO Johnson—a fat-ass little whore from South Philly—came to my cell and opened the door, I smiled.

"Nigga, be strong, and remember, when you get that parole date, I'll be right here picking you up," I said to Mustafa as I walked out of the cell. Music was blaring from niggas' cells on the block, and voices were shouting. It sounded like animals caught in a trap.

"Damn, Rashad! I know you must be happy to be getting out of this place," Ms. Johnson said as we reached the bottom of the stairwell that led to the receiving room.

"I'm good."

"Listen. I know you're probably going to be swimming in some good pussy tonight, but why don't you let a sister help you out? Let me suck the cum out of your balls so that when you get in some pussy, you'll be able to last."

Ms. Johnson was a very capable woman and very tenacious. She dropped to her knees in the stairwell and took my dick in her mouth and closed her eyes in order to concentrate on the sensation. Mmm!" she let out, breathing hot air on my dick. I just looked at this whore sucking and enjoying it all too much. She bobbed her head up and down slowly, letting my dick rest at the back of her throat.

"Cum down my throat, *papi*!" she commanded. She tightened her fist around my shaft and began pumping my shit fast. She gagged when she felt my dick head forcing its way down to her esophagus. When she felt my hot cum dripping down her throat, she smiled. Cum ran from between her lips and trickled down her chin.

"Nigga, I see that you're still hard. You might as well get yourself a shot of ass. My shit is tight. I haven't had any dick since my husband died two years ago. Trust me, I'll have you cumming in minutes!" she said, feeling herself.

"But my people are out there waiting for me."

"Nigga, they waited this long, they can wait a few more minutes. I'll have you out of here in no time." Ms. Johnson opened her pants and dropped them to her ankles. "I'm going to put it in my pussy, Rashad, where it will do me the most good. But first, I want you to fuck my ass. I'm real tight, and so hot you'll cum in a few minutes." She wiggled her ass toward me.

I got behind her and put my hard dick between her firm girlish cakes. I held her waist and slid deep into her sweet tightness. A few minutes in her ass was all that I needed. Once she tightened her ass muscles, I knew that I had no control. I let loose, and it felt as if I was releasing all the stress I had built up inside me into her asshole.

"Damn, that ass was good! But listen. My brother is going to be here for a while. Why don't you take care of him, and I'll take care of you? Write my number down. Whatever you need, you call me. Just let my brother know that I sent you to him," I told her. "Now, let me get the fuck out of here before I get hooked on your ass!"

It took Ms. Johnson ten minutes to process the paperwork. Once I had signed the final papers, she escorted me to the main gate and signaled for the guard in the bubble to crack it open. When the iron gate opened, the first face I saw was Fatima's. She ran up to me and hugged me.

"Damn, nigga! I missed you like you'll never know!" she said.

"I missed you too, baby!" I said as I helped myself to a handful of her soft ass.

"Mr. Lopez, thank you for the good dick!" Ms. Johnson said, winking at me, as the gate began to close.

"Bitch, you had him for a few minutes, if that! But I'm taking him home with me!" Fatima yelled, then turned around and faced me. "Nigga, I know you wasn't in there smashing them Philly whores!"

"Baby, you're crazy! Stop tripping. That bitch is just trying to make you upset. My dick belongs to you only," I said, hugging Fatima tightly. No matter how many guards I had smashed, my ride-or-die bitch would always be Fatima. She rode with a nigga faithfully.

"Nigga, you better act like that dick belongs to me! But right now, we got to get to the airport. Our flight leaves in about two hours. We should make it to Texas by noon, just in time for visiting hours."

We jumped into the waiting car she had rented, and in a matter of seconds, I changed from my prison browns into some street clothes that she had bought me. I felt like a newborn nigga.

Once we arrived at the Philadelphia International Airport, Fatima handed me a stack of cash and said, "At this moment, you can resume your position as my man."

As we walked toward the terminal, I couldn't help but wonder what my mother would say if she found out that I had been locked up.

We got on the plane, and I settled back in my seat and closed my eyes. It was going to be a long flight. The takeoff was smooth, but I kept a tight grip on Fatima's arm. I had never trusted planes. It didn't make no sense to me how they stayed in the air. Any little turbulence and I thought we were crashing. I hated flying. Not until we had landed at Dallas Love Field Airport did I breathe a sigh of relief.

Once we were outside the airport, Fatima took charge. She had arranged for a car to take us to the

Federal Medical Center, Carswell, located in Fort Worth, Texas. The black SUV was waiting for us right outside the baggage claim area. The driver stood outside his truck with a sign that said MR. LOPEZ. That was some balla shit right there.

I grabbed a handful of Fatima's juicy ass. "That's what's up," I said.

The driver opened the car door and took our bags to the trunk. I climbed into the SUV and leaned back in the seat and smiled. I was going to see my mom.

Chapter Twenty-five

Fuck Them Niggas

The South Bronx, the previous day . . .

"Don't run from me, bitch!" Blondee yelled at the young smut bitch whom he was holding hostage in his apartment.

The young girl had learned that there was no escape, and no way to stop the nightmare that she was facing. Her boyfriend had traded her off to Blondee for a debt that he owed. At first, she had thought that Blondee would just fuck the shit out of her and let her go, but three weeks later he was having too much fun tormenting her. Lying flat on her stomach on the floor, her body was shaking uncontrollably.

God, please don't let this crazy-ass nigga kill me! Make him go away! she prayed silently.

Blondee sat on a chair, smoking a blunt. After taking a few hits, his ass was seeing and hearing shit.

"Don't hurt me anymore!" the young girl pleaded. She could see his evil smile, and she peed on herself.

"Look at your stupid little ass, all wet and shit. You pissed on yourself again." Blondee stood over the girl and kicked her in the ribs.

The pain radiated through her entire body, but she kept quiet.

"Bitch, cry! I want you to beg for your life!" Blondee said as he removed the blunt from his mouth and brought it down to the girl's face. He knelt next to her and saw the tears in her eyes. He clenched his teeth and burned her over and over again until he had inflicted twenty burn spots, one for every thousand dollars her boyfriend owed him.

"Please, Blondee! Don't!"

"It's too late for you to be begging, you little bitch." He brought the blunt down to her face again and pressed the tip of it into her right eye.

Suddenly, he heard the door to his apartment being kicked in, and when four of New York's Finest rushed in and aimed their guns at his head, he knew he wasn't hearing shit.

"Police! You bitch-ass nigga, freeze!" a white cop yelled as he felt his finger tighten on the trigger of his Beretta.

The young girl on the floor let out a short sob and gasped for air.

"Make one move and it will be your last!" another cop yelled as he was cuffing Blondee.

Blondee smiled noncommittally. "I'll be out tomorrow morning," he said as he was being led out of the apartment.

The interview room was an eight-by-eight box. The detective observed Blondee through the glass window. He looked relaxed. The detective was ready to make this nigger's life a living hell. The detective took a deep breath and entered the room. He closed the door and took a seat opposite Blondee. The detective's nose twitched at the stench of hot, humid shit.

"Did you shit yourself?" the detective asked.

Blondee slowly turned to look at the detective. "You must be smelling your own damn self."

"I'm Detective Vega, and I want to ask you a few questions. Before we get started, let me inform you that as it stands right now, you are looking at murder one. So I'm advising you of your rights. If you understand them and wish to have them waived, you will have to sign a card to that effect."

"I want to talk to someone with power."

"You can talk to me."

"No. I want to talk to the district attorney, Jimmy Wise. I know who killed his twin sons," Blondee said with no regrets. Going to prison was out of the question for him.

"Sir, do you want an attorney present?"

"No."

"So let's talk, and you tell me what you know. If I think it's credible, I'll get you the DA personally."

A half hour later, Bronx district attorney Jimmy Wise entered the interview room and placed a portable tape recorder on the table in front of Blondee.

Fuck them niggas! I'm not going to jail. Them niggas can't do shit to me if they're locked the fuck up. Maybe now I can take my ass down to Puerto Rico and enjoy my money. I'm about done with the game anyway, Blondee thought as he stared at the tape recorder.

Chapter Twenty-six

I'll Always Love My Mama

Rashad

We arrived at the Federal Medical Center, Carswell, in Fort Worth, Texas, twenty minutes after departing the airport. We were greeted by a black guard, who introduced himself as Officer Jay.

"I'm a good friend of your mother, and I'll be the officer who'll process y'all into the facility, so these other assholes won't give y'all any trouble," Officer Jay said.

I immediately knew this was the guard that La Puta was fucking. The nigga was too friendly.

"Okay, no problem," Fatima responded.

I wasn't really trying to engage in a conversation with a guard. I was still fresh out of jail, and my nuts still smelled like state soap.

Once we were processed, we were led through four metal detectors and a pat-down search. I had just left the pen, and now I was right back in. Even though I was on the other side, it still felt like I was in lockup. The smell was making me nauseated.

The same officer escorted us into the visiting area. I sat in a chair and looked around at all the women who were enjoying their visits, and noticed that I was one of the few niggas in the room.

"Fatima, what's wrong with this picture here?" I asked her.

It seemed as if she was in another world. "What picture? What are you talking about?"

"I'm talking about the people in this visiting room. Look around and tell me how many niggas you see up in here."

Fatima looked around and counted and was surprised to see that there were only five male visitors. "You know why there are only five niggas up in here?" she asked.

"Why?"

"Because most niggas don't have any loyalty toward their woman. When a bitch gets locked up, a nigga finds another hole to stick it in," she responded.

"That's bullshit! I wouldn't do you like that if you ever got locked up."

"Nigga, stop lying to yourself like that! You know that if I were to get locked up with a lot of time, your ass would be ghost in a heartbeat."

"I would come see you every week and would keep your commissary account fat," I said, trying to convince her. In reality, if she ever did get locked up, I would hold her down.

As we were talking, we noticed a number of guards rushing past us into the dressing room, which all the inmates had to enter before being allowed into the visiting room.

"Somebody must be getting it on back there," Fatima said with a smile.

"Damn! What's taking her so long?" I asked her.

Then we noticed an officer walking toward us. It was Officer Jay. "Excuse me. Y'all must come with me," he said with his head hung low.

"What?" I mumbled.

"Sir, we need y'all to come with us," another guard said in a firmer tone of voice.

"Yo, this is bullshit! What the fuck did we do? We went through all them fucking metal detectors and shit. What the fuck did we do?" I was beginning to get upset. Not only was I fresh out of jail, but now I was in a federal jail and was being asked by some federal guards to go with them. I hoped that Fatima wasn't stupid and had not forgotten to empty out her pockets. I had told that bitch to leave that weed alone.

"Sir, we will explain to you what this is all about when we get to my office," a Mexican guard said.

"Man, I came down here to see my mother!" I barked, my voice getting louder with each word.

"Your mother just . . . ," said Officer Jay, trailing off.

"My mother what?" This asshole was doing everything the way he'd been trained to do it, giving me nearly verbatim the police handbook procedure for informing someone that a family member had died. *Build up to it*, the manual instructed. *Don't spring it on them suddenly. Let the family/loved one get used to the idea.*

"Mr. Lopez, your mother just died of a heart attack. We tried everything to resuscitate her. She's dead," Officer Jay said with a sad face. His words hung in the air like moths around a streetlamp.

Fatima turned toward me with her lips slightly parted.

"What is this? Some kind of joke?" I said.

"It certainly is not a joke. She's dead," Officer Jay repeated.

In my life, I'd been through some real tough shit, but I had never experienced the pain I felt when I heard the words *she's dead*.

I cried all the way back to New York. I was inconsolable. Fatima did everything she could to try to soothe me.

"Baby, let me suck your dick. It'll make you feel better."

I shook my head.

"Let me sit on your dick."

I shook my head again.

"Baby, I know it hurts. Let me help you."

I wiped my face. "I just need to be left alone."

Fatima understood. She sat back, put her earphones in, held my hand, and stayed quiet the entire ride.

I never even knew a nigga had that many tears in him. I was hurt, and I wanted the world to feel my pain.

Chapter Twenty-seven

Game Over

Miguelito

Today is the day my nigga is coming home. This nigga is going to be impressed when he sees what I've been able to do with the block. Damn! It feels good to have my nigga back!

I was in my crib, preparing to host my nigga, when I heard the doorbell chime. I went to the window in the bedroom and looked out. A black Ford Crown Victoria with tinted glass was parked in front of my crib. *Stickup boys!* Everything about the car was suspicious. *Fuck!*

I went to my closet and pulled out a .380 and waited. *If these punk-ass stickup boys think they're gonna run up in my crib and jack me for my shit, they got another thing coming! If it's the police, I'm gonna make it real painful for them!*

The doorbell rang again. "Sir, this is the FBI! We just want to ask you a few questions," a female voice yelled through the door.

I took a deep breath, wiped the sweat from my brow, put the .380 back in the closet, and walked to the front door. I opened it slowly. An attractive Puerto Rican woman in a black pantsuit stood at the door. "May I help you?" I asked.

"I sure hope so, sir." She offered me a smile and flashed her badge. "I'm Agent Morales with the FBI. May we come in, por favor?"

"*Para que*? For what? Am I in trouble or something?"

"No. We just want to ask you a few routine questions."

"About what?" I said, stepping aside so the two agents could enter. They stepped across the threshold and stood just inside the door.

"About this individual here." Agent Morales pulled out a photograph of Rashad. It was a mug shot and had to be his last jailhouse photo. "His name is Rashad Lopez, and he was released from prison this morning in Pennsylvania. Have you seen him?"

"No."

"When was the last time you heard from him?"

"Years ago . . . when we were kids," I said.

"You ran in the same gang with him, right?"

"What gang?"

"The Pop Rulers."

"I left that lifestyle alone a long time ago."

"If you happen to see your old friend, let him know that the FBI is looking for him, okay?" Agent Morales said.

I nodded my head. "I'll do that. I'm always willing to help the authorities keep law-abiding citizens like myself safe," I said.

As soon as the agents left my house, I picked up my cell phone and dialed Fatima's number but got no answer. *Where the fuck are those two muthafuckas?*

Chapter-Twenty-eight

America's Most Wanted

Rashad

When I got back to New York, the only thing I wanted to do was strap the fuck up and make the world feel my pain. My mother was dead, and somebody had to die!

Fatima's cell phone kept ringing, and it was fucking irking the shit out of me. "Fatima, will you answer that phone? Or turn it the fuck off, before I break that muthafucka!"

"Nigga, I understand your pain, but you need to understand that I'm hurting too, okay?" she said with tears in her eyes.

Her phone rang about twenty times before she answered it. "This is a bad time."

"Fatima, it's Miguelito. I've been trying to reach you all day!" His voice was stiff and tense.

"Yo, Rashad's mom just passed away."

"I thought y'all were going to visit her."

"We did. We were in the visiting room, waiting for her to come down, when she had a heart attack. Man, Rashad never even got to see her. He's fucked up about it."

"Fatima, I need to talk to Rashad. The FBI came to my house with his photo."

"Stop lying!"

"I'm serious, baby girl. I did some checking, and the streets are blazing. Blondee got popped last night and dropped a dime on the whole squad. He gave up the tapes on the DA's sons' murders."

"Hold up! Let me put Rashad on the phone." She handed me her cell.

"Nigga, what's jumping off? I guess you heard about my mom," I said into the phone.

"My nigga, I feel your pain, but I got some more bad news."

"Miguelito, just give me the news."

"Yo, B, Blondee turned rat. The nigga dropped dime on us about the DA's sons' murders. The Feds are all over the place, looking for you."

"What's the word on the block?"

"Blondee got popped for holding some girl hostage. He got scared and decided to make a trade-off."

"Is he out on bail?" I asked.

"Yeah, but nobody knows where he's at. But it can't be that hard to find his ass. What you want me to do?"

"Come pick me up. Bring the vests and some of them big toys. It's time to declare war on those rat-ass niggas out here. Let them know I'm back on the block."

"Say no more, my nigga. I'm on my way. Till I get there, go online, so you can see your shit on the FBI's list," Miguelito said and then cut off his phone.

I grabbed my laptop, turned it on, and clicked my way to the FBI website. I watched as a page materialized.

FBI's Ten Most Wanted Fugitives
Unlawful flight to avoid prosecution. Double first-degree murder.
Rashad Lopez. Aliases: L
Description:

DOB: July 11, 1985
Sex: Male
Race: Puerto Rican
Height: 5'9"
Weight: 160 pounds
Hair: Black
Eyes: Light brown
Complexion: Light
Build: Husky

Scars and Marks:	Tattoos on forearms
Nationality:	Hispanic
Place of Birth:	New York
Occupation:	Drug dealer, murderer

Remarks: Lopez is an avid reader of urban novels and enjoys strip clubs. He has been known to frequent rap concerts and is a nondrinker. He has demonstrated a propensity for shooting people in the head. Lopez has ties to Philadelphia, Puerto Rico, and the Dominican Republic. He likes to travel to Latin America. He may be in possession of a .380 handgun.

CAUTION. Rashad Lopez is wanted for double murder in the South Bronx. Lopez allegedly shot twin brothers at Orchard Beach. Considered armed and extremely dangerous! If you have any information concerning this person, please contact your local FBI office or the nearest US embassy or consulate. Do not approach this person yourself.

REWARD. The South Bronx DA's office and the City Crime Commission are offering a reward of up to $500,000 for information leading directly to the arrest of Rashad Lopez.

"Fatima, come look at this shit!"

"What the fuck is that?" she asked.

Fatima and I stared at the computer screen in shock. Here I was, fresh out of jail, and already I was America's Most Wanted!

"I finally made the Most Wanted list, baby!"

"Rashad, you act like this shit is funny."

"It is funny, because the only way they're going to catch me is dead. I'm not going back to prison."

"Baby, with a good lawyer, you can beat this case."

"What the fuck are you smoking? They're talking about a double homicide. Bitch, is you crazy?"

"Baby, you can beat this," she repeated.

I was getting nowhere with her, so I changed the subject, getting down to business. "Fatima, I'ma need you to handle my mother's funeral. You know that the Feds are going to be all over it. I got to bounce."

"What are you going to do, Rashad?"

"I'ma become America's worst nightmare! I'ma give the streets of the South Bronx a bloodbath!"

"Baby, please don't go out there tonight!" Fatima pleaded.

"Just handle your business with my mom's funeral. Make sure she goes out like the true queen that she was."

"Baby, please stay here with me tonight!" She wrapped her arms around me and squeezed me tight.

"Fatima, now you're acting soft on me."

"Baby, I just want to spend some time with you."

"Once I take care of business, I'll be staying at the house you got up in Westchester."

Chapter Twenty-nine

America's Worst Nightmare

Rashad

I left Fatima and waited for Miguelito to come through. I had acted tough around Fatima, but for real, I was scared the FBI was watching me. Every sound I heard while waiting for Miguelito made me jump. A dog barking, a phone ringing, someone laughing, it didn't matter. They all got my nerves rattled.

Miguelito's car came around the corner. I knew I had to gain my composure before I got in front of him. Couldn't look like no bitch in front of my boy. I balled my fists. "Time to man up," I whispered aloud to myself.

I hopped in the car as soon as he pulled up next to me.

Miguelito was smiling when I got in. "Yo! It's been a minute. You lookin' swole, my nigga."

"Had to stay fit on the inside. Pull off. We don't need to stay still for too long. Never know who's watching out."

"I heard that." Miguelito pressed the gas pedal.

We got to the safe house, and Miguelito pulled into the garage. Once the garage door was closed, we got out of the car and headed inside. We could finally hug one another. Visions of the hand job I had got from the dude in the joint flashed in my head. I pulled away from Miguelito before I got a hard-on. Didn't need my boy thinking I had been a punk in the joint.

Miguelito had all the arsenal out and was ready for war. There were TEC-9s, Uzis, shotguns. You name it, he had it all laid out in the living room.

Miguelito handed me a shoebox. I lifted the lid and saw that the shoebox was stuffed with cash. I pulled out five stacks worth fifty thousand.

"Just a little coming home present," Miguelito commented.

"Good lookin', my nigga." I hugged Miguelito again. My mind flashed to a shower scene in the prison. What the fuck was going on with me? I released Miguelito. No more hugging him. It was making me feel some type of way.

"Plenty more where that came from," Miguelito said, smiling.

"Yo, what's the news on Blondee?" I asked.

"Nothing solid. But we'll find that snitch. He can't hide forever."

I grimaced. "We got to find his ass. I did my time like a hero, but I just got out, and I ain't tryin' to go back."

"Word. Let me send out some feelers. See what the streets are sayin'."

Miguelito went to the other room to make some calls. I sat down on the leather couch, next to an Uzi, and turned on the television. First thing that popped up was a news segment about the manhunt for me.

"Shit," I said.

I went over to the window and peeked out. The street looked empty, but that didn't make me feel any more secure. I felt the tension in my shoulders rising.

"I got something," Miguelito said as he came bounding into the room.

I turned to face him.

"A nigga I know around the way saw Blondee going into a building on the east side."

"Let's roll," I grabbed a TEC-9 and the Uzi next to the couch. This nigga Blondee was gonna feel my pain. He wouldn't be talking when he was six feet under.

We retraced our steps to the garage and left the safe house. About twenty minutes later rolled up to a run-down five-story building on 168th Street.

"This is it." Miguelito parked the car and double-checked the address on his phone. "My man says he's on the third floor."

I jumped out of the car. I was so anxious to put Blondee to sleep, I ran into the building and up the staircase. As I got to the landing of the second floor, I heard sirens. I looked out the window to the street and saw FBI vans pulling up.

Miguelito came running up behind me. "The Feds are here."

"Motherfucka! We been set up."

We both took off up the stairs. We got to the top floor and pushed through the door and ran onto the roof. The building was surrounded by high rises. We couldn't jump to another roof.

"Stash the guns in the air duct over there," Miguelito said before running to the other side of the roof to find a possible way off the roof.

I opened the air duct and tossed my guns inside. Just as I got the duct cover back on, the door to the roof flew open and I was tackled.

"FBI! Surrender!" The agent yelled, then started kicking my ass.

I fought back as best I could, but six more agents joined in. The COs were nothing compared to these trained assassins. They were putting a hurtin' on my ass. One agent stomped on my leg as I was struggling on the ground. I heard my shinbone crack.

"Ahhh!" I screamed in agony.

An agent got me in a choke hold and started squeezing the life out of me.

"Stop!" I cried.

He kept squeezing.

"I can't breathe."

"Shut the fuck up!" one of the agents yelled and kicked my ribs.

I struggled to speak. "Help me! I can't breathe." My lungs were burning, I was seeing stars, and I didn't want to die. With all my might, I forced myself to say, "I'll tell you everything. Just stop choking me."

The agent who had me in a choke hold let go, and I coughed violently. I held on to my neck and felt the burn where the agent had choked me. I could have sworn I felt blood, like he had broken the skin. When I caught my breath, I sat up.

As soon as I was sitting up, an agent kicked me in my face and knocked me on my back. "Talk, motherfucker!" he said.

I recovered quickly and got back up. I wasn't gonna let them think they could beat me. "Chill. I'll tell you everything."

"You fuckin' snitch!" Miguelito yelled as he came around the corner of the door with his TEC-9 pointed at me. Before the agents could react, Miguelito filled my body with lead.

The last thing I heard before passing out was the agents returning fire on Miguelito.

Chapter Thirty

Purgatory

Rashad

The beeps of the machines next to my hospital bed woke me up. The fluorescent light above my bed shined directly in my eyes. The brace around my neck prevented me from moving my head. When I tried to shield my eyes with my hands, I couldn't move them. I must have been handcuffed to the bed. My entire body felt heavy, like I had an elephant lying on top of me.

A nurse walked in just then. "Oh, you're awake."

The tube that had been shoved down my throat stopped me from speaking.

"Let me get the doctor," she said.

I was unable to move any part of my body while I waited for the doctor. I tried to pick my head up to see what was holding me down, but I couldn't.

The doctor came in with the nurse. He stood next to me and raised the bed so I was sitting up. "Mr. Lopez. It's great to see you awake. You were in a coma for two months. We had to intubate you, so there is a tube down your throat. We are hoping to remove it soon, but we will need to run some tests before we are able to do that. We worked very hard to save your life, and obviously, we were successful. There is some news that I need to share."

He walked down to the end of my bed, gently pulled back the blanket, and squeezed my toes. "Can you feel me squeezing your foot?" he asked.

I saw his hand on my foot, but I couldn't feel it. I shook my head.

"Try to move your foot for me."

I tried as hard as I could, but nothing happened. No matter how much I told my foot to move, it stayed still.

The doctor frowned. He moved to the middle of the bed and grabbed my hand. "Do you feel me squeezing?"

I felt nothing.

"We were able to save you, but unfortunately, a bullet is lodged in your spine, and it is too dangerous to remove it. It severed several nerves and rendered you a paraplegic. Now, there has been a miniscule number of people who miraculously recover from this kind of injury, but the chances are almost zero. I'm afraid you're without the use of your arms and legs and will be confined to a wheelchair for the rest of your life."

I tried to scream and felt the tube rip my throat up.

"Careful," the doctor said. "You don't want to lose your vocal cords as well." He patted my hand, which I didn't feel. "I'm going to have a physical therapist come visit you, as well as a psychologist. This is a traumatic change in your life." He smiled and left the room with the nurse.

Two days later Blondee walked into my hospital room. I was still intubated and couldn't tell him to fuck off. He had a shit-eating grin on his face as he stood next to me.

"Too bad for you. Guess you shouldn't have turned snitch bitch," he said.

I widened my eyes.

"That's right. Everyone on the streets knows you bitched out and told the FBI you was willing to snitch." He laughed. "And now you can't move. Serves you right, motherfucka! You always thought you were better than everyone. Well, now you just a weak-ass vegetable lying in bed, unable to do nothing. Can't even feed yourself. Oh, and Fatima ain't coming by. She don't want to be associated with no snitch. The bitch is smart. She gots to look out for herself and find her a man who can take care of her. Don't worry. I'm not fuckin' the bitch. But plenty other dudes be runnin' up in that pussy. Niggas be turnin' her out!"

He let out a maniacal laugh. He put his hand down my pants and grabbed my dick. He started tugging on it. "See, you can't even get yo' dick hard anymore. Shit, why the fuck even live?" He released my limp dick.

Tears rolled down my face.

"Life is going on without you. Remember that while you're lying here for the rest of your sorry-ass life. There's already a new kingpin on the streets. Sayonara, you snitch-bitch motherfucka!"

After he left the room, I heard his laugh all the way down the hall. I stared at the ceiling, unable to speak or move. Even if I wanted to kill myself, I couldn't do it. I was stuck in hell.

I hated snitches, and for the past few years, my sole purpose had been to kill my snitch-ass brother, and now I was labeled a snitch in the streets, with no way to defend myself. I had gone from a kingpin to a bedpan.

They say that "snitches get stitches," but I got paralysis. I'd give anything to have gotten just stitches.